MW01125793

Always is not Forever

Denise Devine

USA Today Bestselling Author

Forever Yours Series

Book One

Wild Prairie Rose Books

Always is not Forever

Print Edition

Copyright 2024 by Denise Devine

https://www.deniseannettedevine.com

Always is not Forever is a work of fiction. Names, characters, and incidents depicted in this book are products of the author's imagination or are used fictitiously. Any resemblance to actual events, locales, organizations, or persons, living or dead, is entirely coincidental and beyond the intent of the author or the publisher. No part of this book may be reproduced or transmitted in any form or by any means, electronic or mechanical, including photocopying, recording, or by any information storage and retrieval system, without permission in writing from the publisher.

Neither ghostwriters nor artificial intelligence were used in the creation of this book. This entire story is the original work of Denise Devine.

ISBN: 978-1-943124-45-9

Published in the United States of America

Wild Prairie Rose Books

Edited by L. Ness and A. Speed

Let's keep in touch!

Sign up for *Denise's Diary*, my monthly newsletter at:

https://www.deniseannettedevine.com/newsletter

You'll be the first to know about new releases, sales and special events.

About Denise...

Denise Devine is a USA Today bestselling author who has had a passion for books since the second grade when she discovered Little House on the Prairie by Laura Ingalls Wilder. She wrote her first book, a mystery, at age thirteen and has been writing ever since. She loves all animals, especially dogs, cats, and horses, and they often find their way into her books.

She has written twenty-two books, including books in the Beach Brides series, Moonshine Madness series, and West Loon Bay series. Her books have hit the Top 100 Bestseller list on Amazon and she has been listed on Amazon's Top 100 Authors.

If you'd like to more about her, visit her website at:

www.deniseannettedevine.com

Part One

In the beginning…

Minneapolis, Minnesota

Trust in the Lord with all your heart and lean not on your own understanding; in all your ways acknowledge Him and He will set your paths straight.

Proverbs 3:5-6

Chapter One

Early January 2006

Cash MacKenzie had big plans for tonight. Sitting in the top row of the bleachers at Washington High School with his best friend, Ty Owens, he anxiously waited for the basketball game with River's Edge High to start. Last year, the Washington team lost in the playoffs to River's Edge by one point so the rivalry between Cash's school and River's Edge ran at an all-time high. Judging by the barrage of spectators filling the stands in the gymnasium, tonight's game would be more spirited than ever. If their team won, the partying would start before they even left the parking lot.

"I hope you're not expecting any of the guys to join us," Ty announced as he set his varsity jacket on two empty seats to reserve them even though saving seats went against school policy. "I need to hold these spots for a couple of girls." He sat down. "There's someone I want you to meet."

Cash responded with a disinterested shrug. "If I'd wanted to watch the game with a girl, I would've brought my *own* date."

"I'm not fixing you up with a date," Ty argued. "Medley Grant and I are just friends. I asked her to watch the game with me, but she wouldn't agree to it unless she could bring her cousin along too." The sandy-haired linebacker leaned forward, resting his elbows on his knees as he scanned the stream of people filing into the noisy gym. "Her cousin is a sophomore who just transferred here. Medley said she came from some religious all-girl boarding school and she's really shy. Her name is Libby Cunningham."

Cash let out a long groan. "A religious type, huh? That's great. What will we talk about, the Bible?" He took a hefty swig off his bottle of Mountain Dew, wondering why Ty thought he'd go along with this. "I came to watch the game, not babysit a sophomore."

"Medley says that Libby doesn't have many friends yet and she feels guilty about bailing on her cousin," Ty replied with a shrug, rattling on as though he hadn't heard a word that Cash said. "So do me a favor and be nice to Medley's cousin, okay?"

Cash stared at Ty in disbelief. He couldn't imagine what Ty—who only wanted to go to college next year for the parties and the sporting events—saw in a bookworm like Medley Grant. Medley usually hung out with geeky guys who studied all the time and lettered on the debate team! If Libby was as boring as Ty made her out to be, Cash did *not* want to be stuck with her. His buddies on the varsity football team would razz him about it for the rest of the year.

"Ah, c'mon, Cash." Ty laughed nervously, a curly lock of thick sandy hair falling over one eye. "You never pass up a chance to meet a gorgeous girl. You'll probably be a goner when you see her."

"That's not the point." Cash gave him a long, hard look. "There's more to this last-minute setup than you're telling me, isn't there? What gives?"

Ty's face flushed with frustration. "I need you to hit it off with Libby so Medley and I can talk privately. I'm going to ask her out. Help a guy out, would ya? You know I'd do the same for you."

Cash sighed, unhappy about having his loyalty tested. He owed his best friend and football teammate more than a few favors, but why did Ty have to insist on collecting one tonight, when this was such an important game? "Okay," he said reluctantly, "but as soon as you convince Medley to go out with you, my obligation to entertain Miss What's-Her-Name is over."

"Thanks, buddy!" Ty gave him a high five. "You won't regret this."

Cash shot him a sideways glance. "I'd better not."

*   *   *

Libby Cunningham shivered and pulled her fuzzy scarf tight around her neck as she and Medley walked across the icy school parking lot, but the cold January evening had little to do with her discomfort. The thought of meeting Medley's friends made her nervous. Teeth-chattering nervous. Though she and Medley were as close as cousins could be, they were also as different as night and day.

Medley loved high school. She held the title of senior class president and had a seat on the student council. All the girls in her close-knit circle of friends were uber-smart and popular. They were all preparing to graduate this spring—most with honors—and start college next fall.

Libby, on the other hand, hated school and everything about it. She appreciated Medley's attempt to help her fit in, but the trouble was she had nothing in common with Medley's crowd. She could never be like Medley or her friends no matter how hard she tried. Like, what would she say when they asked about her old school?

Hi, I'm Libby Cunningham and I nearly flunked out of two subjects last semester. I skipped class so many times that I got myself kicked out and my father had no choice but to bring me home and enroll me in public school for the rest of the year. Hey, would you like to ditch algebra with me tomorrow?

"Don't be nervous," Medley said in her bird-like voice as she slipped her arm through Libby's. "Ty and Cash are really nice guys. They don't swear or tell rude jokes in front of girls like some of the other players on the football team do."

Libby stopped dead in her tracks. "You didn't tell me we were going to be meeting up with a couple of boys. You know how Grandma Norma feels about that. If she finds out and tells my dad, I'll be grounded—"

Her father believed in a strict no-dating policy until she turned eighteen in her senior year. It was one of the rules he made Libby agree to before he allowed her to transfer to public school. He spent most of his life in Washington, D.C. but her grandmother lived with them, and Norma enforced even stricter rules than him.

"Don't worry." Medley laughed. "I'm not setting you up with a date. Ty and I are just friends. That's all. I promised him that I'd sit with him during the game, but if you're worried about Grandma Norma getting upset, we can always join the girls in my drama club."

Libby grimaced at the thought of trying to fit in with *them*. In her old school, the drama club contained some of the most fiercely competitive and high-strung girls in the school.

"Let's sit with the football players," she suggested, deciding that merely sitting with a boy didn't constitute a *real* date. Sadly, she had no idea what to say to either boy but if the situation turned awkward, she could always fill the time by talking to Medley or reading the romance novel she carried in her purse. Oh, how she loved to read romances! She enjoyed how the heroine always found her knight in shining armor, the love of her life, and lived happily ever after with him.

She usually kept "those kinds of books" in her locker and read them in study hall to pass the time. Grandma Norma didn't approve of such unrealistic nonsense and would throw the book in the trash if Libby brought it home.

Medley tugged on Libby's arm. "Okay then, let's get going. It's cold out here!"

They quickly walked to the entrance of the school and made their way inside. The throng of laughter and excited voices in the gymnasium echoed through the wide hallway, spurring them on. They stopped inside the doorway as Medley perused the brightly lit, two-story arena lined with retractable bleachers, looking for her friends. "There they are," she said as she pulled off her red beret and fluffed her dark, chin-length hair.

Libby glanced around at the huge milling crowd. "Where?"

"Up there." Medley pointed toward a pair of teen boys in the top row of the bleachers. The one on the left stood as soon as he saw Medley's wave. He said something to his friend and the other one slowly stood as well. "Oh, good—they see us. It looks like they're coming down here to meet us."

Libby pulled off her bulky white scarf and matching earmuffs as she looked up. The sandy-haired boy on the left, dressed in a Minnesota Vikings jersey and jeans, enthusiastically waved back. His friend, a tall, broad-shouldered kid with thick black hair nearly touching his shoulders wore a red and black buffalo plaid shirt that hung open over a black T-shirt and black jeans. The kid hesitated as he stared down at her. Something in the intense, almost disbelieving way he studied her made her breath catch in her throat. Had he also been blindsided by this little arrangement? If so, it could explain why he looked so grim. He couldn't even be bothered to fake a smile.

His friend suddenly nudged him to get moving and he began to descend the stairs, never taking his gaze off her. Disappointed by his rude manner, Libby swallowed hard and glanced away.

Wow. He isn't even trying to hide the fact that he doesn't like me. This night is already turning out to be a disaster, she thought in frustration, *and we just got here!*

"I've changed my mind," she blurted and turned her back to the crowd. "Let's go find your drama club before all of the seats are taken."

Medley laughed with surprise. "It's too late. We can't duck out on the guys now, Lib." She placed her arm around Libby's shoulders and pivoted her toward the basketball court. "I get that it isn't much fun being the new kid in school. You'll forget about it once you meet these guys!"

"I doubt that," Libby murmured, wishing the game was already over. All week she had looked forward to hanging out tonight with Medley, but all she wanted now was to get through this wretched game and go home.

* * *

The game was about to start when Ty jumped to his feet. "Hey, Cash, the girls are here," he announced with a grin and waved to someone across the room. "C'mon. Let's go down there to meet them."

Cash slowly rose to his feet and gazed across the gym to the main entrance. The dark-haired one, Medley Grant, wore a long red coat with a matching beret and a black scarf. Next to her stood a tall, slender girl wearing skinny jeans, knee-length boots, and an azure ski jacket. The girl hesitantly looked around as she unzipped her jacket and pulled off her furry earmuffs. She unwound a long, white scarf from her neck as her thick, flaxen hair tumbled to her elbows. She suddenly looked up at Cash, her eyes wide with uncertainty.

Taken by surprise, he stared hard. *Ty was right,* he thought suddenly. *She is gorgeous. And she doesn't look happy to be stuck with me.*

Ty gave him an impatient nudge. "Hurry up." He asked the people sitting next to them to watch his seats and then bounced down the stairs.

Cash shoved his hands into his pockets and followed Ty, hanging back as they crossed the gymnasium floor to meet Medley and her cousin.

"Hey, Medley," Ty said with a sigh of relief as they approached the girls. "I was beginning to worry that you weren't coming. I got here early and grabbed some seats for us."

"Sorry we're late," Medley chirped. "I had to put gas in my car before I picked up Libby."

The meticulous perfection of Medley's makeup and sleek hairdo suggested her tardiness had nothing to do with the dirty business of refueling a car, but Cash kept that little tidbit to himself.

"No problem." Ty stared into Medley's hazel eyes like an adoring puppy so long it became embarrassing—at least, to Cash, anyway. "You're here now."

Cash shook his head at Ty's star-struck theatrics. *It'll never work between these two. They're the equivalent of Shrek and Alice in Wonderland.*

Medley gestured toward her companion. "Oh, this is my cousin, Libby." She turned to the blonde girl. "Libby, this is Ty Owens."

"Hi, Libby," Ty replied enthusiastically.

"Hi," Libby said and absently wound her scarf around her earmuffs as though she found introductions either uncomfortable or boring.

"I'd like you to meet a friend of mine," Ty said as he eagerly motioned to Cash, standing behind him.

Libby's demeanor went from shy to defensive in a heartbeat.

Here we go... Cash thought dismally, wishing he'd never agreed to this.

"Libby Cunningham, this is Cash MacKenzie, the best tight end that the Washington High football team has ever had. In my opinion, anyway!" Ty stepped aside and gripped Cash's shoulder, nearly shoving him forward.

Cash stared at Libby for a few heartbeats, studying her. "Hi, Libby," he said boldly as his gaze bore into hers. "It's nice to meet you."

She responded with a guarded nod.

Excuse me, Cash thought, wondering what her problem was.

Ty glanced at the gymnasium clock. "Come on, let's take our seats or we'll miss the jump ball."

They climbed the stairs to the bleachers, Ty first then Medley and Libby. Cash took up the rear. They squeezed into the narrow space reserved for them just as the home team got the ball and the chase began.

Cash stared at the players racing down the court as his mind slipped into a daze and the scene began to blur. He'd been waiting in anticipation of this game for a week. Why then did he feel so distracted?

The light, sweet scent of her perfume wafted in his direction, pulling him even farther from the action on the floor. He leaned forward on his knees, struggling to concentrate, but no matter how hard he tried he couldn't seem to focus on anything except the silent, beautiful girl sitting like a statue next to him, giving him the cold shoulder.

Chapter Two

Libby sat rigid as a post as she pretended to stare at the game even though her mind couldn't be farther from it. Why had she let Medley talk her into this? Hanging out with these guys made her realize how inadequate and out of place she was. They were smart, popular, and accomplished—everything she was *not* and never would be. Though she tried not to glance around, she couldn't help but notice that other students were staring at her. Was her discomfort that obvious?

Cash sat so close to her that she could barely breathe. Even the slightest move could cause their bodies to touch. To make matters worse, every time she glanced at him, she caught him looking back at her.

Why does he keep staring at me? Does he realize that I'm totally freaked out because I don't belong here?

His leg bumped against hers. "Sorry," he blurted as he turned toward her looking deeply into her eyes. "I—I wasn't trying to—"

Pushing her jacket off her lap, she wedged it between them on the seat. "It's too crowded in here. And too warm." The words tumbled from her lips before she could stop them, making her sound like a whiney, immature brat.

"Yeah, it is," he said, agreeing with her. "And stuffy, too. Up here, you can see a lot, but I'd rather be closer to the action down there," he said, pointing to the seats near the floor.

Was that a hint that he didn't want to be stuck in the nosebleed seats with her? Embarrassed, she turned away and pretended to concentrate on the game.

They didn't speak again until halftime.

Ty rose from his seat. "I need to stretch my legs." He turned to Medley. "Would you like some hot nachos with cheese?"

"No thanks," she said as she grabbed her purse and stood up. "A bottle of water would hit the spot for me."

"Okay. Let's go," he said cheerfully with his hand extended, motioning for her to go first.

Wait—you can't leave me here with him, Libby thought, panicking as she jumped to her feet to make room for them to pass. She started to suggest that they all go together, but stopped short when Ty grabbed Medley's hand as she squeezed past. She smiled. "Bye."

Libby didn't answer. She turned away frantic at being deliberately left behind to keep company with Cash MacKenzie.

*   *   *

"See you later," Ty said to Cash as he and Medley took the stairs.

Cash stood with Libby in awkward silence, glancing everywhere but at each other.

"Would you like something to drink?" he asked, desperate to get out of this embarrassing situation. "We could get a Coke or something."

"I already have some water." Libby pointed to a bottle tucked into her jacket pocket. "But thanks, anyway."

"Would you like to take a walk?" he said quickly, not knowing what else to do. "Get some fresh air?"

She shrugged and stared at the floor, as though she didn't find his

16

suggestion to her liking, but then she surprised him when she said, "Um...yeah, okay."

"Great," he said, relieved. "Let's go."

They made their way down the bleachers and left the noisy gym, heading into the main hallway. Medley and Ty were nowhere to be seen. Walking away from the crowd, they ventured down a wide corridor lined with metal lockers. "Ty said you transferred here from another school," Cash stated, desperate to start a conversation. "Where did you come from?"

"Challendorn Christian Academy."

"I've never heard of Chall—er...that place. Ty said it was a private school."

She nodded. "It's exclusively for girls. It's in Illinois."

"Wow, that's a long way from home," Cash said. "Medley told Ty that you've been here for two weeks, but I haven't seen you around."

Libby stared at the polished stone floor. "I transferred during Christmas break."

She wouldn't look at him, but at least he was getting her to respond. "How do you like it so far?"

She hesitated. "It's...it's okay, I guess."

"Oh," Cash said, wondering why he had to coax her to talk. Obviously, she didn't care for Ty's last-minute matchmaking schemes, either, but they were stuck keeping each other company until halftime ended so he asked her another question. "Do you live far from school?"

"My house is across the street from Lake Harriet."

Really? Cash thought in surprise. *Her parents must have money. That's one of the most expensive neighborhoods in Minneapolis.*

He knew it was none of his business, but his curiosity got the best of him. "Why did you transfer? Didn't you like it there?"

She shrugged.

"What does that mean?" He waited for her explanation, but she said nothing.

"Look," he said, growing tired of trying to draw conversation out of her. He stopped, jamming his hands into his pockets. "I'm sorry Ty and Medley ditched us. I don't like it either. Ty wanted some private time with Medley, but if you'd rather go back to the gym to find your cousin, then go."

She blushed at his directness. "I'm sorry too. I didn't mean to be rude. I'm—" She took a deep breath and lowered her gaze again. "I'm just nervous. I—I mean, I don't know what to talk about because I've never been in a school with boys before. I've gone to private girls' schools and girls' summer camps all my life. Besides," she said, suddenly looking up, "it's no fun to be around someone who doesn't like me."

Her admission stopped him in his tracks. "What are you talking about? I never said that."

She drew in a tense breath and folded her arms, glaring at him. "You don't have to say anything. Your attitude is enough."

He met her angry look with a pointed stare, challenging her. "Maybe I'm just reacting to you. It's obvious that you don't like *me*."

"I never said that…" she replied, lobbing his claim back at him.

"So, we're even. Now what do we do about it," he said in a softer tone as he moved closer. "I say we start over." He grinned and extended his hand. "Truce?"

Her eyes widened at his offer. She hesitated as if thinking it over but then slowly extended her hand. "Okay…"

As he gently slid his palm around hers, the softness of her skin distracted him. "Um...great." He blinked, trying to pull his thoughts together. "I really would like to keep walking, but if you're more comfortable going back to the gym where we're surrounded by people, we'll turn back."

"Let's keep going," she replied eagerly as she slowly let go of his hand. "The gym is too noisy, and the air is fresher here. I'd rather walk for a while."

They strolled along the corridor in the opposite direction of the gym. The clamor of people faded into blissful quiet except for the soft padding of their shoes on the polished stone floor.

Now that things had settled down between them, Cash couldn't help studying her. She had the most beautiful hair he'd ever seen. Thick and silky, her straight golden locks tumbled down the back of her long sweater. Curious, he wanted to take in every inch of her but knew it would be rude and forced himself to pull his gaze away.

"I didn't like all of the strict rules that they forced on us," she said suddenly.

"What do you mean?"

She gave him a serious look. "You wanted to know why I transferred."

Her answer didn't make sense to him. "Why did you go to that school if you didn't like their rules?"

She looked up, her pretty face darkened by a troubled frown. "I had to because my dad... It's complicated."

He took that as a hint to mind his own business.

After a moment, she added, "Medley told me that Ty is a linebacker on the varsity football team, and he introduced you as a tight end. Do you miss the season now that it's over?"

He smiled, relieved to find common ground. "Yeah, I love

19

playing football. Do you like the game?"

At the mention of sports, she brightened. "Yes, I love to watch live sports, especially football. I can't wait to watch the Superbowl," Libby replied with a small giggle. "My dad promised to take me to the winter Olympics in Turin, Italy this year, but it didn't work out."

"Hey, that's too bad," he remarked as they began to walk again. "The Olympics would have been a great experience. What happened?"

Her tense sigh gave him the feeling he shouldn't have asked.

"Something came up and he had to stay in Washington, DC," she replied with a grimace. "It happens a lot."

"What does your dad do for a living?" Cash asked curiously.

"He's a politician."

"Wait..." Cash stopped. "You mean Senator Frank Cunningham is your *dad*? He's the chair of the Senate Intelligence Committee! I don't pay much attention to national politics, but I do know who he is because he's from Minnesota. He's a pretty powerful guy in Washington."

"Maybe so," she replied, "but unfortunately, it means I see very little of him. To make up for cancelling on me at the last minute, he promised to take me to a Colorado ski resort for a long weekend instead. We'll see."

The sadness in her crestfallen expression tugged at his heartstrings. "What about your mom? At least you have her, don't you?"

"No." Libby shook her head. "She died from an aneurysm when I was five years old. My dad hasn't remarried so my grandmother lives with us and manages the house."

"Well, your dad is lucky he had someone to step in and take over," Cash said, trying to find a bright spot in the conversation.

"That's what Grandma Norma tells him every time he upsets her." Libby's eyes flashed with anger. "She does her best to make sure *I* never forget it, either."

Libby's indignation suggested things weren't going well at home. He'd decided to steer away from the subject of her family and talk about the Minnesota Vikings instead when suddenly they heard a door open and shut in a nearby corridor. Cash turned in the direction of the noise and realized they were close to the faculty lounge. The room used to be unlocked all the time, but last week, someone sneaked into the lounge and stole valuable equipment, making this area off-limits to students and visitors now. If someone on the faculty saw them together in this part of the building, there would be consequences.

"Come on," he said to Libby, "we need to get out of here fast."

Heavy footsteps approached. Cash glanced around in panic. He didn't care if a teacher caught him roaming an area off-limits, but he didn't want to get the senator's daughter into trouble. He tried the closest door—the library. To his surprise, it opened without a sound. He grabbed Libby by the hand and pulled her inside, shutting the door as quickly and quietly as possible. They waited in the dim room until the sounds died away, but as Cash turned to leave Libby walked toward an alcove and sat in the window seat, staring at the nearly full moon.

"Let's go, Libby. We need to get away while the coast is clear." Her cream-colored sweater would be easy to spot if they encountered another teacher coming out of the lounge.

She stared out the window as though she hadn't heard him. "I like to come here during my study period and sit in this spot while I read. The sun feels good on my face."

The wistfulness in her voice made her sound lonely and he wondered why. Distracted by her mood, Cash walked over to the alcove and sat down beside her. "What are you thinking about?"

She pensively stared through the glass. "How much I'm looking forward to spring. I don't like the isolation of winter. Especially after school. I hate going home to an empty house."

21

Moonlight beamed through the window, casting a silvery sheen across her flawless skin. He watched her innocently stare at the stars and realized he wanted to know more about her—a lot more. She shivered from the cold coming off the glass.

"You must be freezing, sitting next to this window." He slid his arm around her shoulders, his senses sharpening when an unexpected surge of warmth filled his chest. He'd never experienced such a deep sensation with a girl before and didn't know what it meant, but knew he never wanted it to go away. "Is that better?"

For a moment, Libby's eyes reflected confusion. Then she smiled and leaned into the crook of his arm as though becoming drawn to him, too. The sparkle in her clear blue eyes drew his gaze to her full lips. Before he realized what he was doing, he lowered his head and placed his mouth upon hers. She froze at first, as though unsure of what to do. Then she awkwardly kissed him back. The sweetness of her soft mouth sent his emotions into a tailspin.

His heart melted into a puddle at her feet.

Ty was right. I am a goner...

Cash reluctantly pulled away. "We'd better get going before we get into trouble for sneaking in here. If anyone caught us here in the dark…" He wanted to spend the rest of the game alone with her, but it wouldn't be wise to tarry and risk discovery. As they rose, he took her hands in his. "I know we've just met, and you may think I'm rushing things, but…is there any chance I can see you again? Like, could we meet for pizza after school?"

The light in her eyes dimmed. "I can't."

Disappointment crushed his euphoric mood, but the unhappiness in her voice became his main concern. "What's the matter? Do you already have a boyfriend?" He lifted her chin and saw her eyes glistening. "Is that why you're crying?"

"My dad says I'm not allowed to date until I turn eighteen." A tear sped down her cheek. "That's two whole years from now! You might as well forget about me."

The suggestion disappointed him. His mind spun, searching for a solution. He gently slid his arm around her, pulling her close. "Look, we'll find a way around it, okay? So, we can't date; we can still be friends. We'll find a way to see each other after school."

She pulled away. "I don't see how that could work. We'll only be able to meet for an hour or so."

"Trust me, okay? I need to see you again, even if it's only for a few minutes. We'll find a way to be together." He gazed into her eyes and knew he never wanted that *goner* feeling to go away. He didn't know if he'd fallen in love at first sight or if this rush would be a distant memory by tomorrow, but tonight the giddy sensation in the pit of his stomach had him hooked.

She suddenly threw her arms around his neck and kissed him—hard. He froze, momentarily stunned by the realization of how much she wanted to be with him.

"I've never kissed a boy before," she whispered breathlessly. "I always wondered what it would be like. It's amazing." She laughed. "I can't wait to do it again."

Smiling at her sense of humor, he pulled her close, making her wish his command.

Chapter Three

The next day at school, Libby wandered the hallway that she and Cash had explored the night before, clutching her English workbook and desperately hoping to meet up with him before class. She'd never met anyone like him. His self-confidence, broad sense of humor, and love for sports fascinated her. She'd never talked to a varsity football player before, either—much less *kissed* one. Last night he gave her the impression he wanted to be more than just friends. Did he still feel that way today? She needed to find out.

She spotted Ty Owens dumping his backpack on the floor with a heavy thud before proceeding to open his locker. "Hi, Ty," she said, hurrying toward him. "Have you seen Cash?"

Ty straightened his thick, muscular frame and tossed a book into his locker. "No, but he usually races into the parking lot about the same time I do." Ty checked his watch. "Five minutes before class."

"Oh..." The thought of Cash barreling through the heavily patrolled parking lot alarmed her. "I hope he doesn't get into trouble. Isn't speeding against the rules?"

Ty merely grinned.

The five-minute bell rang. Libby's hopefulness began to fade. She needed to get moving to make it to her first-period class on the other side of the building.

Disappointed, she started to walk away. "Okay, see you later."

"Libby!"

The urgent tone in Cash's deep voice made her heart leap with joy. She spun around and caught her breath. He sauntered toward her wearing jeans, a gray flannel shirt, and a black leather jacket that hung open, revealing his wide, muscular chest. His rugged grin and bold stance suggested his attitude could use an adjustment; his kohl, wavy hair needed more than a trim, but no one had *ever* looked so good to her.

"Hi there..." His eyes shone with attentiveness meant only for her.

"Hi," she replied with a smile, nervously clutching her workbook.

Their gazes melded and for a few moments, the bustle of students slamming lockers and rushing past them to class faded as they stood together, caught up in their own little world.

He cleared his throat. "You've been on my mind ever since we said goodbye last night."

Her stomach fluttered at his confession. "I've been thinking about you, too."

All the way to school, she'd rehearsed in her mind what she wanted to say, but the moment she gazed into his cocoa-colored eyes, she couldn't recall a single word. All she could think about was how she'd frozen up at first when he kissed her last night. Inwardly, she cringed, feeling stupid. Though she'd purposely tarried in the library to get to know him, she hadn't expected him to make such a bold move. Since then, she'd thought about nothing else. She wanted to kiss him again to show him she liked him and that he made her feel special in a way no one else had ever done before.

He waved to Ty, though he kept his focus on her. "May I walk you to class?"

"I'd love that. I have English this period." The aroma of his spicy cologne surrounded her, distracting her even more than her thoughts did. "Where are you going?"

"I have psychology," he replied as he hung his jacket in his locker and dumped his backpack.

"If you walk me over to my class and then come back here to yours, you'll probably be late."

He slammed his locker door and fell in step with her. "Ah, don't worry about me. I'm getting an A in Mrs. Benson's psych class. I'll just tell her I left my notebook in my locker and had to go back for it. She'll let me off with a lecture."

Libby laughed, but her happiness stemmed from being with him rather than what he said. She couldn't stop smiling. "I had a great time at the game with you last night."

A group of girls congregating in the hallway stared at her and exchanged whispers as she passed by, but she ignored them, focusing only on Cash. "I hope you did, too."

"Yeah!" His face lit up with a huge smile. "That was a great game, wasn't it? Especially the second half. We trampled the River's Edge Otters. We're in first place!"

A tall, blond boy raised his hand as he passed, smacking palms in a high-five with Cash.

"Ty didn't have the greatest night, though," Cash continued. "He got super bummed out when Medley told him she liked him only as a friend." His wry tone suggested he knew Medley would dash Ty's crush on her. "He wasn't happy when we showed up after the second half started, either. I heard about it later."

26

Libby laughed again. "I noticed that. He looked a little grumpy, didn't he? He didn't seem to enjoy the game after that, but *I* did."

Too soon, they arrived at her class.

"I'm glad we got the chance to meet up again. I almost missed you," Libby said as they stood outside the door. She knew she sounded silly, but she couldn't think of anything else to say.

"Me, too, but I wish I would've gotten to school earlier. We've barely had time to talk." He looked deeply into her eyes. "Let's meet up after school."

A twinge of guilt gave her pause. Her father meant it when he said *no* to dating boys.

But he didn't say I couldn't have friends...

Her spirits lifted. "Okay, where?"

He thought for a moment. "Do you know where Sandhill Nature Center is?"

She nodded. "My family has been a patron of the center since it was built."

"Okay," he whispered in her ear so that no one but her could hear him. "I'll meet you at the interpretive center at four o'clock."

The final bell rang. Libby scurried into her classroom but stopped briefly inside the door, giving him a big smile and a quick wave.

*   *   *

The gray sky and biting cold dampened Cash's already somber mood as he parked his car in the empty parking lot at the nature center and shut off the engine. Slumping against the headrest, he exhaled a frustrated sigh. This morning, standing with Libby at the door to her English class, a nagging little voice in his head whispered that he was making a colossal mistake by getting involved with her. At the same

27

time, his heart disagreed. Instead of listening to the voice of reason, he'd shoved the thought away and hurried to class. That nagging little voice in his head, however, had persisted all day, turning into a five-alarm warning over getting involved with Libby Cunningham.

He couldn't deny he wanted to see her again. At the same time, however, he knew he'd made a mistake in succumbing to his feelings. Feelings were fickle. Common sense was not, and he'd allowed his attraction to exceed good judgment once he saw her walking away from his locker. He knew he had to back off this relationship and the more he thought about it, the faster his reasons for doing so stacked up like dominoes.

"She's not allowed to go on dates yet," he said aloud to rehearse why they needed to be friends and nothing more. "I like her—a lot—but this is an exercise in futility." He gripped the steering wheel and stared at the tall, wooden gates separating him from the nature center grounds. "Even if she could go out with me, she's too young to hang out at the parties I go to and given the strictness of her old man, the last thing I want to do is get her into trouble with *him*."

He pulled out his keys and opened the car door. "I'm going to be eighteen next month and I'll be free to do whatever I want. I shouldn't be messing around with a girl that I can't even take to a basketball game," he grumbled to himself as he swung his leg outward and climbed out of the car. He slammed the door and trudged toward the entrance. "I should be looking for a job for next summer," he said with a sigh, "not wasting time sneaking around with a girl I just met." He shoved open the gate. The place looked deserted. "I need to tell her straight out and get this over with…" He stared through the glass door of the interpretive center, hesitating as his gaze fell upon Libby. Something about her pulled at his heartstrings and, as before, his resolve began slipping away.

Libby sat by herself at a small round table wearing burgundy jeans and a fuzzy pink sweater with a book opened in front of her. Her thick golden hair cascaded past her elbows like a veil of rich silk. She

28

rested her chin on her hand and stared at the wall opposite her, looking sad and alone. It troubled him to see her so unhappy. He yearned to slide his arms around her and kiss away the pain of loneliness in her eyes.

That still, small voice in the back of his mind urged him to turn around and go back to his car, that she'd eventually get over it if he stood her up, but he didn't move. He remained there, torn between his intention to break off their friendship and his desire to comfort her...

Suddenly she looked in his direction and recognized him, giving him no chance to turn back. He pushed against the door and went inside. Green carpeting, wooden tables, and chairs filled the cheery, window-lined space.

"Hi!" She burst into a smile and slid out of her chair, her eyes sparkling as he approached her. "I'm so glad you're here. You had me worried that you weren't coming."

"I always keep my word," he said, gazing down at her, his voice echoing in the empty room. "I stopped at Best Buy to look at notebook computers and lost track of the time. I need a new one for my classes at the university next year."

He'd intended that statement to lead into his "I want to be friends only" speech, but she cut him off and changed the subject.

"You're so lucky, Cash," she said, placing her palm on his chest. "It must be awesome to have such great plans for your life."

Her statement surprised him. "Everyone should have some kind of plan, don't you think? Don't you have any?"

Her smile dimmed. She shook her head. "Not really."

"Why not?"

"I don't know." She shrugged. "I guess I'm waiting until I turn eighteen and can take charge of making my own decisions. I'm just trying to get through the next two years one day at a time."

He slid his hand around hers. The softness of her slim fingers entwined with his distracted him, but he focused on the seriousness of her words. "There must be something you're looking forward to..."

"Well, sort of," she said curtly, "but I doubt it will ever happen." She looked up. "I wish my dad would meet someone special and get married. Then I'd have a complete family again and my grandmother wouldn't have the last word about everything I say and do. She might even *move*."

He blinked with surprise. "You hate her that much?"

"Well, I don't hate her, but sometimes I wonder if she hates me. I sure don't like her as a substitute for my mother. She's too strict and she always uses her religion as a weapon whenever she gets upset with me." Libby grimaced, making a face that clearly indicated she had no time for her grandmother's harsh views.

Her negativity regarding the concept of religion gave him pause. He usually didn't get into sensitive matters like that with girls, but he'd never encountered anyone before who'd complained so bitterly about it.

"My parents are religious, too, but I don't have a problem with them," he said. "I don't practice Christian values like my mom wants me to. Actually, if she found out about some of the stuff I've done, she'd be pretty upset, but that doesn't mean I'm against her faith—or her."

"I'll bet she doesn't use it against you every chance she gets!" Libby's eyes suddenly narrowed with resentment. "You'd hate it like I do if you were told every day what a bad person you were in God's eyes just because you didn't measure up to a set of impossible standards. After a while, you'd stop trying, too."

"Hey, hey, take it easy," he said softly. "You're not a bad person." He pulled her into his arms, resting his cheek against the top of her head. He took a deep breath, inhaling the sweet, floral aroma of her hair. "You're one of the nicest girls I've ever known."

"I'll bet I'm the only *nice* girl you know who you can't take on a date." She sniffled. "Will you meet me here again tomorrow after school?"

He knew it was now or never. He had to tell her, even though his heart didn't want him to say a word. "Libby, I—"

"We're closing in five minutes!" The voice echoed through the open half-door of the interpretive center offices.

Cash looked at the large round clock on the wall. It read 4:25 pm. He let his arms drop to his sides. "Come on, we need to go. I'll give you a ride home."

Libby glared in the direction of the voice that disrupted their discussion. She slammed her book shut and shoved it into her backpack as the lights began to shut off, one by one.

"Was that your algebra book?" Cash held her coat to hurry things up, helping her slide her arms into it. She zipped it closed and then hastily wound a long, thick scarf around her neck.

"Yeah," she said in a bored tone. "I need to study because I'm getting a D minus in the class." She gave him a look of pure frustration. "I mean…I just don't get it."

They scurried out of the center into the waning light and climbed into Cash's car to escape the frigid temperature.

"I'm cold," Libby said, shivering.

Cash revved his engine to warm it up faster. "Does that help?"

She moved closer to him and smiled. "A little."

He wanted to kiss her again. Sitting so close to her gave him ideas that he knew, if acted upon, would complicate things in a major way. He revved the engine again and stared out the windshield, purposely putting emotional space between them to lessen the temptation.

In a couple of minutes, the heater began to generate warm air.

Cash shifted into gear, anxious to drive her home. He needed to talk to her and make it clear he wanted only her friendship so they could both get back on track with their lives.

Turn upon turn, she directed him to a house situated across the street from Lake Harriet, a monstrous red brick building with white trim, three dormers protruding from the gabled roof, and a towering brick chimney at each end. A pair of concrete lions positioned at the end of the front sidewalk looked like sentinels guarding the grounds. Instead of pulling into the driveway, she instructed him to drive past it and park a block away.

He pulled into a tree-lined spot in front of a stucco house with a mass of bare vines covering the brick chimney and left the car running. As he drove past, he didn't see any lights shining in her house and began to wonder why Libby needed to be so secretive about her activities.

He turned to her, sliding his arm along the back of her seat. "Why didn't you want me to drop you off at home?"

She clutched her backpack and looked at the floor, as though his question embarrassed her. "I told you. I can't date boys until I'm eighteen."

"Yeah, but we're not dating. We simply met at the nature park after school *as friends*." There, he'd said it. "Why all the sneaking around?"

"Because I..." She looked up, distress clouding her eyes. "Because my grandma..." She sighed. "You wouldn't understand."

He knew better than to get involved, but her reaction concerned him. He leaned close. "Yes, I would. Try me."

She stared out the passenger window for a moment, as though contemplating her answer then turned back to him and looked deeply into his eyes. "My grandmother says I'm not allowed to even talk to boys, much less be friends with them. She believes it's sinful because

I'm flaunting myself and that kind of behavior will lead to worse things." She gave an angry, defiant laugh. "Why do you think I showed up at the game with Medley? Grandma would only allow me to go if Medley picked me up and gave me a ride home. I'd planned to hang out with Medley all night—that is until Ty introduced me to you. If it hadn't been for Ty's crush on Medley, I would never have known what it was like to be with you. And kiss you." She beamed, her face instantly brightening. "I've never kissed a boy before. It was awesome!"

He blinked in disbelief. "You mean to tell me that you've honestly *never* been with a guy before? You've never been kissed by anyone but me? When you told me that last night, I thought you were just kidding."

She shook her head.

Cash froze, his emotions spinning. He remembered sensing her hesitation when he kissed her, but he'd never attributed her reaction to inexperience. Instead, he'd assumed it was because she'd expected him to ask her permission first. Realizing he'd been the first boy in her life to share a kiss with her and hold her close gave him a startling surge of protectiveness...and possessiveness.

He wanted to be with her more than ever but hesitated, knowing if he went down that road and gave in to temptation, it would be impossible to come back. Preoccupied with uncertainty, he didn't realize he'd angled his head and leaned close until she mistook his intentions and threw her arms around his neck.

"I don't want to be with anyone else, but you, Cash."

He gazed into her eyes, powerless to resist. Nevertheless, he needed some answers. "Why me? Why not another politician's son or someone from a family with money and influence, like yours?"

Her smile widened with joy. "Being with you makes me so happy. You make me feel good about myself. I can tell you feel the same. We were meant to be together."

33

He couldn't deny it. She'd described the innate elation he fought so hard to reject every time he saw her. He slid his arms around her tiny waist. "You're the sweetest girl I've ever known," he whispered and drew her close. As his mouth covered hers, he knew that from this moment on he'd never be the same again.

Before things escalated further Cash forced himself to pull away. "I've got to get going," he said and drew in a deep breath as he untangled her arms from his neck.

She looked disappointed but quickly recovered with a smile. "Will you meet me again tomorrow after school at the nature center? Help me with algebra?"

Dazed by his internal struggle, he nodded. "Okay. I can do that. Algebra comes easy for me."

"That is so awesome. Thank you! See you tomorrow!" She gave him a quick kiss on the lips then gathered up her backpack and shoved open the car door.

Cash watched her run down the block, making sure she arrived home safely, all the while wondering how he'd fallen for this girl so hard and so fast.

Chapter Four

Mid-January

Libby paced the floor of her bedroom, waiting for her grandmother to leave the house. She had big plans for tonight, but they couldn't unfold until Norma went to her campaign committee meeting.

"I'm leaving now," Norma shouted.

Libby hurried out of her room and leaned on the newel post at the top of the stairs, looking down.

Norma Cunningham stood tall and stately at the base of the wide oak stairway, dressed in a brown tweed business suit, her black wool coat and scarf draped over her arm along with her pocketbook. "Is your homework finished?"

"I'm working on it," Libby replied, using her standard excuse. So far, she'd only finished algebra. Cash had helped her with her assignment at the nature center before they took their usual walk on the trail around the marsh.

Norma's gray eyes narrowed behind her gold-rimmed glasses. "Get going on it *now* and stay off the telephone. I want you to be in bed by nine-thirty. Is that clear, Olivia?"

Libby pursed her lips and nodded obediently, holding her anger inside. She hated her formal name. The only person who used it always combined it with some manner of reprimand or criticism.

Norma slipped into her coat and scarf and then plucked her black cloche hat off a marble-topped console table, pulling it down over her short, white hair. "I'll be back around ten-thirty." Her keys jingled as she pulled them from her purse. Moments later, the automatic garage door rumbled as it rolled up. The kitchen door slammed.

"Thanks for wishing me a good night," Libby murmured as she turned away. From the window in her room, she let out a sigh of relief watching Norma's black Town Car emerge from the garage and back out into the street. Once the car drove out of sight, she twirled around, happy to have the house all to herself, but more importantly, to have all evening to spend with Cash!

Humming a tune, she danced into her walk-in closet and shuffled through dozens of garments, looking for just the right outfit. A few minutes later, she emerged from the bedroom in black velour leggings, a sparkly blue top and knee-length boots. She spun around in her full-length mirror, checking to make sure her outfit looked perfect.

The clock downstairs chimed the half-hour. Time to meet the most special person in her life! She touched up her makeup, swiped sparkly pink gloss across her lips, and then left her room. She bounced down the stairs and hurried through the kitchen then bolted through the back door into the backyard to unlock the gazebo.

The gazebo, a fancy name for their guest house, had once served as an open-air structure, but now resembled a miniature Victorian home. Only the cupola on the shingled roof and gingerbread on the wooden screen door remained a testament to the original structure. The building had been enclosed and upgraded with a wet bar, a murphy bed, heat, air-conditioning, a full bath, and a secure phone line.

Libby removed the key from the saucer of the large flowerpot next to the door and shoved it into the lock, but the door opened easily. Did someone forget to secure the building the last time they used it?

Concerned, she shoved on the door...and froze.

Franklin Cunningham sat on a high stool at the bar with his back to her, wearing a hand-tailored navy suit, and discussing a campaign matter with someone on the phone as he scrolled through his notebook computer. A draft of frozen air flowed into the room, prompting him to turn around.

She quickly shut the door, shivering from the cold—and the prospect of having her secret discovered. "D-Dad, what are you doing here? Why didn't you tell me you were coming home today?"

He frowned instead of answering but signaled to her to take a seat and wait for him to finish his call.

She quickly wiped off her lip gloss and nervously chewed on the inside of her cheek as she sat stiffly on a loveseat and glanced at the clock on the wall. Her palms began to moisten. Cash had agreed to meet her at six-thirty. He should have been here by now. She desperately hoped something had caused him to be late!

Frank continued his conversation, leaving Libby to stare at his back and wonder if a campaign event had instigated his sudden return. She perched on the edge of the loveseat and studied his tall frame. He looked thinner than the last time she saw him. The dark circles she'd immediately noticed under his green eyes suggested stress-induced fatigue. Small smudges of silver collected at his temples, looking out of place with his light brown hair. She hated to see how much the pressure of his political career had worn him down, but even more so, how much it took him away from her.

Frank cut his conversation short and hung up. "Hello, sweetheart," he said softly, as though seeing her took away every care in his world. He stretched out his long arms. "You look nice tonight. What's the occasion?"

"Oh, nothing," Libby answered with a shrug, attempting to downplay her appearance. "I wore this to school today." A lie, but it served her purpose.

"Well, come here and give me a hug. I've missed you."

Libby sprang from the loveseat and joyfully wound her arms around her father's neck. "How long have you been home? I didn't see your car in the driveway and Grandma didn't say anything to me about it."

He smiled wearily as they slowly pulled apart. "Mother doesn't know I'm home yet. I flew in a couple of hours ago and caught a cab at the airport. I came in through the alley so as not to disturb anyone in the house."

He often arrived home unannounced and instead of coming into the house, spent time in the gazebo—his private sanctuary. Libby understood his need for privacy because of his job but couldn't help harboring hurt over his deliberate attempt to delay making his arrival known. It prompted her to question whether he'd planned to tell her at all. It also made her wonder how many times he'd come and gone without her knowing he'd even been there.

She smiled and stared into his tired eyes. "How long are you going to be home? Can we go to breakfast tomorrow? Can we, Dad? I don't have school because it's Martin Luther King Day."

Frank gave one of her long, blonde locks an affectionate tug. "I'm sorry, honey, but I have an early business meeting and then I'm flying back to Washington."

Her happiness plummeted. "Okay..." she replied slowly, struggling to contain her disappointment. "You'll be back in time for our ski trip next weekend, though, won't you?"

He flinched, as though bracing himself to deliver news he knew she wouldn't take lightly. "Something has come up. We need to reschedule."

Libby gasped. "You're cancelling our trip?" She backed away, crushed that he would treat this promised weekend with such low priority. "Why? You know how much I was looking forward to skiing in Colorado with you."

He remained calm, even though his rigid posture revealed his regret over disappointing her. "I'm scheduled to be in Washington for a special briefing with the President. It's at his request," he said in a soft, even voice, "and I need time to prepare. I know how much you were counting on this trip. We'll get there, I promise. I'll have my assistant reschedule it as soon as things settle down."

"But...things will never settle down. There's always a new crisis every week." Her voice rose to a whine, as though she was still five years old, but she didn't care. His unavoidable change of plans had destroyed her trust in his ability to fulfill future promises. "We've been planning this weekend ever since you cancelled our trip to the Olympics."

Frank placed his fingers under her chin and lifted her face to meet his gaze. "I'm sorry, Libby. I understand how you feel. I'm not happy about it, either, but it can't be helped."

The phone rang, putting an end to their conversation. Frank's attention switched to the incoming call, his demeanor quickly changing. "I have to take this," he said in a serious, business-like tone and snatched the phone, placing his palm over the receiver. "We'll talk later." He turned his back to her again and began conversing with someone from Washington. That much she could discern given the stark change in his tone. Those people in Washinton were always his main priority!

Libby stormed out of the gazebo into the cold and looked around for Cash. She didn't see him and worried he'd bailed on her, too. She ran into the house and grabbed her coat then slipped out the side door and passed through the garage to the front of the house. Down the street, Cash's car sat idling in front of the house where he usually dropped her off. She rushed to the passenger side and jumped in, shutting the door quickly behind her. He sat with his hands on the steering wheel, as though he'd planned to leave.

"I'm so glad you're still here!" She pulled off her coat in the toasty warm interior. "I didn't see you at the gazebo, so I thought maybe you'd changed your mind."

Cash stared at her with a look of uncertainty. "I made it to that little house in your backyard around six-thirty, but when I reached the door, I heard you inside talking to someone. I figured I'd better get out of there before I got caught. I didn't want to get you into trouble." His brows knit together. "What's the matter? You look upset."

Suddenly, tears began to flow down her cheeks. "That was my dad," she said, her voice cracking. "He came home earlier tonight, but he went straight to the gazebo and didn't tell us he'd arrived. I think he'd planned to stay in the gazebo all night working and leave in the morning without even telling us he'd come home."

Cash sat back, releasing his hands from the steering wheel. "Libby, it's not the end of the world just because your dad had to work."

She shook her head. "He backed out of our trip to Colorado."

Cash put his arms around her and held her close. "Hey, I didn't mean to sound like a jerk. I know how much you looked forward to going. I'll make it up to you someday. We'll go there together."

She looked up, seeing him through a watery blur. "You're the only one who never lets me down. I wish we could be together all the time."

"We're together now..." he murmured as he reached up and gently slipped a lock of hair behind her ear.

Cash was the only person who acknowledged how unhappy she was—the only one who truly cared about her feelings. He was her refuge from a life of always trying to measure up; always falling short. He didn't ignore her or judge her the way her family did. He didn't judge her at all.

40

Libby threw her arms around his neck and pulled him down on the seat as she began to kiss him, desperately wanting him to make her unhappiness go away.

* * *

Cash drove home in a daze, his mind churning with confusion. He hadn't planned for things to get out of control; he was only trying to console her. He didn't count on her tears affecting him so deeply that he couldn't resist her, but he got caught up in the heat of the moment and he went too far.

Drawing in a tense breath, he gripped the steering wheel, regretting his impulsiveness. That said, he didn't regret the way she'd made him feel—his feelings for her were stronger than ever now, but in his heart, he wished they hadn't crossed that line because now they could never go back.

We're playing with fire, he thought as he pulled into the driveway of his parents' home and shut off the car. *What happened between us stays with us, but if somehow her father found out...*

Frank Cunningham wielded a lot of power in the Senate. He wouldn't take kindly to having his authority tested in his own home. Cash could care less about Cunningham's wrath upon him. He could take care of himself, but he worried that if the senator found out about them, Libby would be the one to suffer. She'd most likely be sent away again to a school like the one she just came from. Cut off from her entire family. And it would be his fault.

"I need to talk to her," he murmured to himself. "We need to put some space between us for a while to let things cool down." He knew that the more time he spent with her, the harder it would be to stop sharing intimate moments with her. Putting their relationship on hold for a while was the hardest thing he'd ever had to do, but he saw no other way to protect her.

He went into the house through the back door and double-checked the time. Libby said her grandmother wouldn't be home until around ten-thirty, a half-hour from now. The kitchen contained an old-fashioned wall phone with a long cord; long enough to stretch into the back porch and shut the door.

His parents were in the living room watching the evening news. Cash pulled the business card with Libby's home phone number scrawled on it from his wallet. He picked up the avocado-colored handset and punched in the number then backed into the porch and softly closed the door.

She answered on the second ring.

"It's Cash," he said in a low voice. "Can you talk?"

"Yes! My grandma isn't home yet," she burst out, nearly cutting him off. "Oh, Cash, I'm so glad you called. I haven't been able to stop thinking about us—about tonight and…and…"

The wistfulness in her sweet voice pierced like a knife through his heart. Closing his eyes, he inhaled a deep breath. He didn't want to hurt her, but he had to do this. "Libby, about tonight." He swallowed hard. "You and I… What I mean is, I think we should—"

She abruptly cut him off. "I know. We need to be extra careful from now on. But tomorrow is a slam dunk. My dad will be back in Washington and my grandma has another fundraiser," she replied with a thread of excitement in her words. "We can meet again. In the gazebo."

Heat rose up the back of his neck. He knew what would happen if they were there alone. No, this couldn't wait. He needed to break it off *now* before he changed his mind. He cleared his throat. "That's not a good idea. What if your grandma came home early and caught us together? I don't want to get you into trouble—"

"Don't worry, whenever she goes to one of those things, she's never home until late," Libby snapped, cutting him off. "No one is going to find out about us." She went silent for a few moments. "You sound like you don't want to be with me anymore."

She gave him the perfect segue to tell her the truth, but suddenly his mind went blank. Leaning against the wall, he stared numbly at his feet, realizing he was losing his nerve. Besides, he reasoned, he needed to tell her in person to make her truly understand. "All right," he replied slowly. "I'll be there tomorrow night. Same time."

"Oh-oh. I just heard the garage door rolling up," Libby said quickly. "I have to go. I can't wait to see you again tomorrow!" She made a kissing sound and hung up on him.

*   *   *

The next night, Cash arrived at the gazebo at six-thirty sharp, apprehensive but determined to tell her the hard truth and leave before he had time to change his mind. The door opened as soon as he walked up the steps, as though Libby had been looking out the window for him. Wearing black jeans and a long red sweater with a shiny black belt, she quickly pulled him inside and shut the door.

"It's freezing out there," she complained with a shiver as she unzipped his jacket and slid her arms around his chest. "Warm me up!" Her face and hair glowed in the softly lit room. Her eyes sparkled as she gazed deeply into his eyes. His heart began to thud.

He suddenly realized the mistake he'd made by coming here. He intended to push her away, but his arms disobeyed him and slid around her waist instead, pulling her closer. "I can't seem to stay away from you even though I know we shouldn't be together," he whispered as his resolve crumbled. "I came here tonight to put our relationship on hold, but now that we're together, I don't think I can…"

Her face paled; her expression froze with shock as she pulled back. "You were going to break up with me? Oh, n-o-o-o. You can't do that. I won't let you!" She paused, her lips quivering. "I'm so glad that

43

you changed your mind!"

There was no use in denying it to himself any longer. "There's something about you… When we're together, I'm so happy I don't want to let you go. I think I'm falling in love with you, Libby."

She slid her hands up his chest to his face, pulling it close to hers. "I know what you mean. Being with you makes me so happy that I forget about what makes me sad. I've never been in love before, but I *know* this is real. I've already fallen in love with *you*."

He pulled her close and kissed her with all his might.

Chapter Five

Late May

When the dismissal bell rang at the end of the last period, Libby sprinted out of the classroom, waving goodbye to her classmates as she headed for her locker to dump her class materials, homework included. With finals a mere week away, she needed to study, but with so much on her mind right now, she couldn't concentrate. Why did the last few weeks of school always seem to be the hardest? She couldn't wait to leave her sophomore year behind!

On her way to board the school bus, she ran into her cousin. "Hi, Medley, are you going to the Cunningham family picnic this Saturday at Como Park?"

Medley wore designer jeans today with a hot pink blouse. Her dark, chin-length hair ruffled in the humid, May breeze. She said goodbye to a couple of classmates and turned to Libby. "Yeah," she said in what sounded like more of a groan than a word. She rolled her eyes, as though the idea of sitting around a gritty cement picnic table at a park pavilion and listening to a bunch of old-timers reminisce about the "good old days" held no appeal for her. "My mom has been baking like crazy all week."

She doesn't know how lucky she is, Libby thought wistfully as she listened to Medley complain about cleaning up a mountain of dishes every night. Grandma Norma didn't cook or bake anything anymore. She had Delores, their cook and housekeeper to do it all for her.

Oh, how Libby wished her mother was still alive! What she wouldn't give to spend an evening baking cookies or decorating a cake with her. "Do you want to explore some of the trails down by the lake on Saturday?" she asked Medley, pushing the sad thought away. "It'll give us an excuse to get away for a while."

Medley's hazel eyes brightened. "Absolutely," she replied with sudden enthusiasm. "I love Como Lake! I'll bring my walking shoes. Mom says about a hundred people are coming. Is Cash going to meet up with you there? With that many people, he could easily blend in with the crowd. Grandma Norma wouldn't know who he was."

Libby had no idea whether Aunt Barbara would say anything to her father if she saw Libby hanging out with a boy, but Norma would raise a huge fuss and inform Frank *immediately* if she spotted Libby and Cash together. Libby would probably be grounded on the spot.

"Um, no... He's not coming. Perhaps another time," she said, keeping her voice light and cheery to sound as though it didn't matter, even though she found it disappointing.

She gripped the shoulder strap of her purse and pulled it off her shoulder in a futile effort to ease the constant weight of guilt pressing upon her, but it didn't help. Norma had been crankier than usual, losing her temper and snapping at Libby for the smallest of mistakes due to the pressure she'd been under ever since Frank's poll numbers dropped a few points. With his reelection coming up in November, she'd worked day after day with his core campaign committee to strategize ways to bring his numbers back up and keep the trend going. He was still ahead in the race, but Norma wasn't happy about the sudden change.

To add insult to injury, Libby's third-quarter algebra grade had sent Norma into a rage. Her grade continued to improve now that she had Cash to help her with her homework, and she was passing, but with only a C+. According to Norma, in an election year, everything mattered, including her academic record because low or mediocre grades would reflect badly on her father.

The lecture had cast a pall over Libby's already low morale, especially her feelings of worthiness. Norma never missed an opportunity to let her know that a lousy performance indicated she hadn't tried hard enough, and God didn't condone laziness. The Bible said that lazy people ended up with nothing. She'd grown up hearing that God disapproved of her behavior and consequently, she'd always felt unworthy of His love.

Desperate for acceptance, she'd found the approval she craved in Cash. He had proven to be the hero she'd always dreamed of and more...much more. His reputation as a tough athlete drew popularity and respect from his male peers in the senior class, but his bad-boy attitude and dark, sultry looks were irresistible—especially to the girls in school. Why, then, had he chosen to bypass the girls his age and pursue a sophomore who wasn't even allowed to date?

Because, Libby thought defiantly, *we were made for each other. We belong together.*

Waving goodbye to Medley, she boarded the bus, anxious to get home. She planned to meet with Cash at Sandhill Nature Center tonight and the sooner she arrived, the more time they had to spend together. She had something important to share with him and she couldn't wait to tell him.

*   *   *

Cash arrived first at Sandhill Nature Center and stood inside the entrance gate next to a tall, fragrant lilac bush, watching people come and go as he waited for Libby to arrive. Earlier that day, she'd stopped him on his way to class and said she had something important to talk to him about, but he didn't have a clue as to what she wanted.

47

They had little chance to speak during the day. Their only opportunity to see each other and talk most days came *after* school. Even then, Libby only had about an hour of free time. Her grandmother expected her home for dinner every night at five o'clock sharp. The only opportunity they had to meet in private was when Libby could get away and meet him in the gazebo.

The tall, wooden gate creaked open, and a small group of people swarmed into the entrance area. Libby trailed behind them wearing white jeans and a pink T-shirt with a V-neck, her long blonde hair covering her arms and shoulders. The moment she saw him her face lit up with a smile and she flew into his embrace.

He slid his arms around her and pulled her close, not caring today who might be watching. "Hey," he said in a deep, throaty voice, "I thought about you all day today. Couldn't wait to get through my classes so I could see you again. I've missed you."

"The hours dragged by for me, too, Cash." She gazed longingly into his eyes. "I can't wait until we can be together *all* of the time."

He pulled her behind the lilacs and pressed her against the bark of an old oak tree. His palm slid up her arm, the tips of his fingers tingling with desire as they caressed the silky texture of her skin.

"Cash..." She grabbed his hand, twining her fingers around his as she pulled it away. Her eyes widened with anxiety. "We need to talk."

Uneasiness began to seep into his mind. Something was wrong. "Okay, so, what did you want to tell me?" he asked, trying to sound casual.

"Not here. Let's take a walk."

Gripping her hand possessively, he guided her toward a shaded gravel path that led away from the nature center and deep into the forest, out of the presence of curious onlookers. "Is it the same reason that you marked up my yearbook this morning before school with a cryptic note about sharing some kind of secret with me? Every guy in the first period who saw it asked if you were letting me know in code that you were planning a *hot* date." Hopeful, he gazed down at her with a grin. "Were you?"

"This isn't funny, Cash. It's just..." She gazed up at him with an anxious frown on her face. "I mean...I..."

"I know what's on your mind," he replied softly as he stopped walking and slid his arm around her. "You're still upset because you can't come to my graduation party next week. Look, you know I don't even want one if you can't be there, but I don't have a choice. My mom is planning the whole thing and she's turning it into a major production."

Libby shook her head at his best guess and continued to stare at him, her worried frown deepening.

His uneasiness grew into deep concern. "What is it? Did somebody rat on us to your dad?"

She pulled his long, sinewy arms around her and gazed into his eyes. "Would you marry me tomorrow if you had the chance?" Her voice shook as though she feared he'd say no.

Instead, he tightened his arms around her, pulling her close. "I'd marry you right now if I could. Libby, you know how much I love you. I want to tackle every guy who so much as looks in your direction. You're all I've ever wanted."

Libby's gaze searched his. "Would you love a child as much if we had one?"

He shrugged. "I guess so, but that's a long way off..."

She gave him a trembling smile. "Um...maybe not."

"*What?*" He went rigid at the warning in her voice. A chill slid down his spine. "What are you talking about?"

Her smile disappeared, her eyes blinking rapidly with

nervousness. "I'm pregnant."

The words hung in the air like a bad joke.

Cash slowly let go of her, his jaw dropping in shock. "Wha...what did you say?"

Her smile trembled. "I'm going to have a baby!"

He stared at her lips as she spoke, his mind processing the words in slow motion. After a few moments, he responded, his voice sounding hoarse and unnatural. "Um...are you sure? How do you know?"

Libby's face crumpled at the disappointment in his voice. Tears pooled in her eyes.

"Hey, hey, take it easy," he heard himself say. "It's probably just a false alarm."

She shook her head as the tears flooded her cheeks. "The home test shows a positive result."

"Yeah...but...." He blinked, barely able to grasp the seriousness of her confession. "We've only been together...without protection...once. How could it happen so easily?"

She sniffled and then cleared her throat. "I'm—I'm not an expert on this, but I think it *can* happen on the first time. I've been feeling nauseous and exhausted for a while now. That's why I took the test."

Cash blinked furiously, his thoughts swirling into a blur of confusion. His arms fell to his sides as an emotional numbness overtook him.

Libby...pregnant? No, that can't be...

He released a sigh of unease. "Are you sure? I mean, I heard my mother talking about it on the phone once with my aunt. Those things aren't always accurate. Maybe you should get another test and try it again—"

"Cash, it's correct." She placed her palms on his chest, her blue eyes flashing with anger. "I'm going to have a baby. *Your* baby. You're going to be a father! We're now a *real* family. Aren't you happy?"

"If this is what you want then I'm happy for you, but...but...this is all so sudden." He anxiously wiped away the sweat beading on his upper lip. "My parents are going to have a fit when they hear about this. For that matter, what's your old man going to say?"

She folded her arms with an air of defiance. "Maybe he doesn't need to know."

"Wait," Cash said staring at her in puzzlement, "um... Are you saying that you want to get an—"

"I'm saying that if we just...I mean, if you and I... If we went away together, we wouldn't have to tell anybody."

"That's not a good idea." He shook his head at such a ridiculous suggestion.

Her hopeful look turned into a glare of disappointment. "Why not?"

"We'd never get away with it, for one thing," Cash argued. "Your father would probably send the cavalry after us. I hate to think of what he'd say to *my* parents when he found out we were on the run."

"What *can* he say? I'm going to have his first grandchild sometime next October. You're eighteen now and you can get a full-time job to support us. He'll have to give me his blessing to get married."

Married? Even though he'd just admitted that he wanted to marry her, the realization of such a daunting responsibility—unleashed upon him without warning—washed over him like a tsunami. In one instant and with two simple words his life had spun out of control; his world had changed forever. The uncertainty of his future scared him. He blew out a tense sigh and stared at the ground as he ran his hands through his hair. "We can't just run away. We need to tell our parents what's going on

51

with us and hope they understand. It's the only option we have."

"Dad should be home from Washington sometime in the next two weeks." She gazed up at him, fear clouding her face. "He's going to be upset when he finds out. He'll be hurt that once again I've disappointed him." Libby's eyes spilled over with fresh tears. "I want you there with me when I tell him. I can't face him alone."

He didn't want to think about breaking the news to Senator Cunningham that he'd been seeing the man's daughter against his wishes and worse yet, made her pregnant, but he couldn't expect Libby to approach him on her own. She needed a strong ally to stand against a father who'd ignored her all her life and a hard-nosed grandmother who would show her no mercy.

Libby's sobs brought his thoughts back into focus. He hated to see her cry. Drawing her into his arms again, he held her close. "Don't worry, honey. Everything is going to be okay. I'll be with you every step of the way. I promise." He gazed down at her as his gaze melded with hers. "We'll get through this—together."

*   *   *

Libby sat next to Cash in his car at a convenience store several blocks from her house. "I'd better get going." She grabbed her purse off the floor, wishing they didn't have to keep their relationship a secret. Once they told her dad about the baby, however, that would change. "I'm due home right now."

Cash gripped the steering wheel as he turned to her. His deep, cocoa-colored eyes perused her with tender concern. "Do you want me to drive you home?"

"No, no," Libby said, opening the door part way. "I'll simply be late."

He placed his hand on the back of her neck, pulling her close. "I'm worried about you. Are you going to be okay?"

"I'll be fine." She touched her forehead against his, dropping her purse on the floor again and sliding her arms around his neck. "I want you to come over on Saturday night. I'll slip out through one of the French doors and meet you in the gazebo at midnight."

His lips covered hers, confirming the date with a long, passionate kiss. "No matter what happens, I'll always love you," he murmured and then grinned. "Both of you."

Libby didn't know whether to laugh or cry. She wanted to have a baby as much as she wanted to be with Cash forever, but knowing everyone else would react to her news with anger and condemnation made the road ahead of her a difficult one.

After a long moment, she reluctantly pulled away and grabbed her purse again. "I wish we were meeting tonight, but Grandma is hosting a group of ladies from Dad's campaign committee, and I have to serve refreshments."

He gave her a puzzled look. "Isn't that what your housekeeper should be doing?"

"Yeah," she said and blew out a frustrated sigh, "but Grandma says it's important for Dad's image to have his family involved in his campaign, so I have to be there."

Cash leaned one arm along the top of the steering wheel. "Okay, I'll see you on Saturday then."

Clutching her purse, Libby kissed him once more and shoved the door all the way open. "Bye."

She climbed out of the car and grimaced at a cramp that suddenly gripped her lower back. Sitting in such a tight space never used to bother her, but now, at four months pregnant, it made her back start hurting almost immediately. But then, other things bothered her that never used to as well.

As she walked home, the thought of her grandmother finding out about Cash *and* the baby had sabotaged her jubilant mood. Grandma's religious beliefs held very strict views on intimate relationships outside of marriage. Thus, she had been the influencing factor that led Libby's father to say no to dating boys or even hanging out with them.

She hastily removed her earrings and shoved them into her jeans pocket as she crossed the backyard of her house. With a quick swipe of her fingers, she also wiped away her eyeshadow. Grandma disapproved of makeup, jewelry, and trendy clothes because, in her words, they tempted boys to harbor impure thoughts toward young ladies.

She stopped at the back door, twisted her flowing hair into a ponytail, and then stepped into the kitchen.

Norma stood in the middle of the room, giving instructions to Delores, their housekeeper. Norma's tall frame, clad in her signature look, a black business suit, and crisp white blouse, matched her authoritative air. She turned at the creak of the door opening and glared at Libby. "Where have you been? Your dinner is on the stove, getting cold."

"I lost track of time—"

"That's inexcusable and I don't want to hear it ever again, young lady. Olivia, why must I always remind you to be more responsible?" Norma's face turned crimson against her gold-rimmed glasses and short white hair. "Our guests will begin arriving in about ninety minutes and you still need to shower and dress properly. You can eat later. Go upstairs and get ready!"

Libby marched out of the room before Norma could see her angry expression. She hated it when Grandma called her by her legal name and treated her like a child; she hated it even more when Grandma talked to her like a child—an unwanted one.

"Why does she always have to be so mean to me? What did I ever do to her?" she whispered to herself as she ran up the stairs to her bedroom overlooking the street. "If Mom were alive, I know she

54

wouldn't allow Grandma to treat me like that!"

She looked down and placed her hand over her abdomen. "Don't worry, little one," she said, "I'm *never* going to talk to *you* that way."

She went into her room and collapsed on her bed, planning her escape on Saturday night.

Chapter Six

Memorial Weekend

On Saturday morning, Libby and Grandma Norma met Medley and her parents, Barbara and Bob Grant, at the open-air pavilion on the shore of Como Lake in Como Regional Park in St. Paul. Some people had already arrived, grabbing all the shady spaces in the parking lot and setting up their family picnic tables. Most everyone brought comfortable lawn chairs and decorated their tables to spend the day in style.

Libby and Medley were immediately put to work, setting up the event. Three hours later, they approached Barbara.

"Mom, we're tired. It's eleven–thirty and we haven't had a break since we got here," Medley complained as she and Libby collapsed at their picnic table, protesting the numerous jobs assigned to them while the other cousins their age weren't helping at all.

Three tables closest to the kitchen had been set aside for snacks, salads, and desserts. Crockpots and electric roasters filled with fried chicken, barbeque meatballs, and casseroles lined the long serving counter connecting the picnic area to the pavilion's kitchen.

"We want to take a walk around the lake before it gets too hot," Medley said. "Can we go now?"

Medley's attitude surprised Libby. Her cousin normally sounded perky and upbeat, but this time she came across as almost whiney. At any rate, it worked, because Aunt Barbara, an older version of Medley—tall, thin, hazel eyes and short dark hair—nodded her consent as she sampled one of Great Aunt Violet's freshly baked chocolate chip cookies.

"All right. You girls did a great job," Barbara said enthusiastically as she brushed cookie crumbs off her khaki shorts and white polo, "but your Uncle Bernie is going to give a short greeting along with the blessing in about a half-hour so be back here by then."

The girls cheered and smacked their palms together, making a high-five. If they walked at a brisk clip, they could circle the small, tranquil lake and be back in time. Medley had begun to pull on her walking shoes when Norma appeared.

"Clara needs someone to slice buns while she's carving the ham," she said abruptly. "Olivia, will you please go into the kitchen and help her out?"

Libby turned to Norma and struggled to keep the disappointment out of her voice. "But Medley and I have been working in the kitchen all morning. We want to take a walk around the lake—"

"There will be plenty of time for that after lunch. Clara needs assistance now." Norma nudged Libby in the direction of the kitchen. "Do as you're told and take Medley with you. She's expecting both of you."

Medley turned to her mother. "*Mom...*" she said pleadingly, "you said we could go."

Barbara placed her hand on the picnic table as if bracing herself for a confrontation. "Mother, the girls have done more than their share of the work and I've given them permission to take a short break before we start serving. I'll find someone to help Clara or else I'll do it myself."

"Nonsense, you're spoiling these two! If Frank were here, he'd agree and settle the matter." Though she forced a smile for appearance's sake, Norma's voice held no warmth.

Barbara's fingers clenched around a serving spoon and Libby knew from experience the issue suddenly had nothing to do with her or Medley any longer, but rather her grandmother's constant comparison between a son who'd become a very powerful man in Washington and the daughter who'd disappointed her mother by marrying a lowly middle-class accountant.

"*Mother*," Barbara said slowly, dragging out the word in a steel-soft voice, "the girls have worked hard, and *I said* they could take a break."

Her grandmother countered with a grim stare. "We'll discuss this later." Without another word, she spun away and charged toward the kitchen, probably so that no one within hearing distance would get wind of the ongoing tension simmering between her and her only daughter. Norma considered the family reputation to be of utmost importance because everything that negatively affected the family eventually affected her son's political career. Her dedication to him came first— always. Unfortunately, his accomplishments had raised the bar so high that no one else in the family could ever hope to measure up.

Medley glared at her grandmother's retreating figure, waiting until Norma disappeared into the kitchen then turned to Aunt Barbara. "May we go now?"

Barbara nodded, her silence indicating that her thoughts were still focused on the disagreement.

Libby and Medley helped themselves to bottles of water from the cooler and left the pavilion, running toward the lake. They had even less time now.

The bright midday sun glistened on the crystal blue water of Como Lake. The gentle flapping of a Mallard duck's wings made a soft whooshing noise as it eyed them curiously along the shore. The stress

Libby encountered back at the pavilion slowly ebbed away.

"What a pretty sight," Medley exclaimed as she slowed to catch her breath. "I wish we could just sit here along the shoreline and eat our lunch, don't you?"

"Yeah." Libby gazed across the water of the small, still lake. "It's so peaceful here." She looked at her cousin. "No uptight people to ruin the day. Just you and me."

Medley laughed. "I guess you see this kind of beauty every day, though, living in a mansion across the street from Lake Harriet."

Libby shrugged, embarrassed by the stark difference between her house and Medley's family home. She lived in a three-story, six-bedroom, Georgian Revival home in the heart of one of Minneapolis' most expensive neighborhoods. Her father employed both a housekeeper and a gardener to maintain it. To outsiders, Libby appeared to have a charmed life with every advantage she could possibly want. No one except Cash and Medley's family knew how much she truly lacked.

"I was thinking," Medley said as they walked along, "that we should spend some time together this summer. I'm on the waiting list for art camp, but in the meantime, we could plan a picnic or two at Lake Harriet or just hang out together at the beach, you know?"

"That would be great." Libby took a deep breath, taking in the fresh air. "If you don't get into art camp, what's your plan for the summer after school lets out next Wednesday? Are you going to get a job?"

Medley stopped on the walking path and tipped her head toward the sun, closing her eyes to soak up the warmth. "I've applied for a part-time receptionist opening at my dad's office. How about you?"

"I'm not sure..." Libby replied cautiously. "It depends on how I feel."

Medley stared at her in puzzlement. "Why is that? Are you ill?"

Libby's gaze darted along the blacktop walking path, making sure they were alone. "If I tell you a secret, do you promise not to tell anyone else?"

"Of course—you can trust me!" Medley exclaimed. "What is it?"

Libby drew in a deep breath. "I'm going to have a baby."

Medley covered her gaping mouth with her hands as she emitted a loud gasp. She took her hands away and pressed them over her heart. "Are you serious? I had no idea that you and Cash— Does he know you're pregnant?" At Libby's nod, she blinked several times in astonishment. "How did he react?"

"He said he loved me, and he promised me that we'd get through this together."

Still clutching her heart, Medley blurted, "What are you going to do?"

"Keep a low profile until my dad gets home." The thought of telling her dad frightened her. Libby folded her arms to keep them from shaking. "Then...then Cash and I are going to break the news to him together."

"Oh, Libby," Medley squeaked, sounding ready to cry. "You're too young to be saddled with so much responsibility. You'll miss out on so much. This changes everything!"

"Don't feel bad for me," Libby said and placed her hand on Medley's shoulder in a sincere attempt to console her. "Don't you see? Now I'll finally have a family of my own. I'll have someone to love who loves me back. I won't be alone anymore."

Medley's confused frown indicated she didn't quite see it that way. "Are you saying that you're going to get married? But Lib, you're only sixteen. It's a mistake!"

"It's better than going home every night after school to a big, empty house, having a dad who's pretty much a stranger to me and a grandmother who treats me like I'm nothing but a burden. I'm a cross she has to bear for her son's sake!" Libby shoved her hands into the pockets of her shorts and tried to swallow the lump forming in her throat. "I know it might seem crazy to you, but I just want to be happy. For the first time in my life, I have a chance to experience what everyone else takes for granted. Things will work out for the best. I'm certain they will."

Medley didn't try to hold back. Tears pooled in her eyes. "I know it hasn't been easy for you. I've always wondered what it would be like to live in that huge house and have a father who has so much money, but honestly, I'm glad you're getting away from that place. Cash had better treat you well or he will answer to me!"

"Cash is my true soul mate. He doesn't expect me to be perfect," Libby said and began walking again. "And he doesn't judge my mistakes like Grandma says God does. Cash *understands* me."

"Why do you say that?" Medley wiped her eyes as she fell in step with Libby. "God isn't judging your mistakes. He knows what you're going through, and He cares."

"Oh, yeah? Then why hasn't He answered my prayers?" Libby snapped. "For years, I've been begging Him to give my father a special person to marry so Dad would stay home and our family would be complete again, but God has ignored me." She let out a deep breath, becoming angry. "God doesn't approve of the way I act so why would He bother to bless me?" As always, guilt and unworthiness settled upon her like a heavy yoke, deepening the hollow spot inside her. "I've always been told that I'm a disappointment to Him." She stared at Medley. "I gave up trying to win His approval a long time ago."

"I'm sorry you feel that way, Libby, and I hope someday you change your mind." Medley placed her arm around her cousin's

61

shoulders. "I'm going to pray for you, anyway, and ask God to bless you with a healthy baby and a loving family. Whatever the outcome, I hope you receive the happiness you've always wanted."

*   *   *

Cash waited in the gazebo until twelve-thirty on Saturday night before deciding he should give up on Libby. He figured her grandmother must have stayed up late to watch a movie or had invited some of her political cronies over for a meeting, making it difficult for Libby to slip away.

"I'll give her five minutes more," he murmured to himself as he glanced at the illuminated dial on his watch. "If she doesn't show up by then, she probably isn't coming so I'm out of here."

Cash reclined on the pillow-soft loveseat and tried to stay awake, but the relaxing atmosphere of the tiny getaway made it difficult to resist closing his eyes. He understood why Senator Cunningham often used the gazebo as a place to retreat from his family.

He lay in the dark, listening to the soft, methodical tick-tock of a wall clock and mulling over what to tell the Senator about his and Libby's situation. Lately, he'd taken to watching Frank Cunningham in action on C-SPAN in committee hearings to observe him. The Senator, though always soft-spoken and diplomatic, exuded confidence and authority while grilling people to extract the information he sought. Though Cash had never seen the man lose his composure or even raise his voice, would the Senator maintain control when he found out his only child had gone behind his back and...

The door suddenly opened, waking him with a start.

"Cash?" Libby sounded upset, awakening him as the words penetrated his sleep-fogged brain. "Are you still here?"

He jerked to a sitting position so fast the momentum threw him off balance and he nearly rolled off the cushions. "Yeah, and I've been waiting forever," he mumbled, rubbing his eyes with the heels of his hands. "What time is it? I must have fallen asleep."

"It's twelve forty-five. I'm sorry I'm late." She shut the door and turned on a small light, then padded across the room and sat next to him, pressing her forehead against his shoulder. "I'm not feeling well."

"What's wrong?" He turned on a small light on the end table and lifted her chin, studying her face in the dim light. She looked unusually pale tonight with dark circles under her eyes. It worried him. "Hey, are you going to be okay?"

"I think I ate something at the picnic today that didn't agree with me." She closed her eyes and groaned. "Somebody brought bruschetta and it was scrumptious, but I ate too many. I shouldn't have scarfed down those little franks in barbeque sauce either. They were spicy and really greasy, but they tasted so good I just couldn't help myself."

He wrapped his arms around her and held her close. "Bruschetta, huh? Yeah, I can tell. You smell like garlic." He chuckled. "I won't stay long then. You need to get some rest. No more rich food for you." Reaching up, he tucked a wisp of blonde hair behind her ear. "I suppose that means you can't have any pizza then. I brought one and two big bottles of Coke, but it looks like I'll have to take care of your share."

She jabbed him with her elbow.

"Ouch! What's that for?"

"That's what you get for bringing me something I can't eat," she countered teasingly. "I could smell it the moment I opened the door." She wrinkled her nose. "The smell of pepperoni makes my stomach queasy."

He began to tickle her.

"Don't, don't!" she cried and shoved his hands away. "I can't laugh. It makes my stomach hurt."

63

"Sorry, I didn't mean to make you feel worse," he said sincerely. "Do you mind if I dive into the pizza then? I'm hungry."

Libby shrugged as she pulled from his grasp and leaned back against the sofa, closing her eyes. "I guess so."

Cash jumped up and grabbed the pizza box on the coffee table. He flipped the top open and the aroma of pepperoni filled his nostrils. "M-m-m-m...." he said as he reached into the box and grabbed a slice. It was cold now, but it still tasted great to him.

He opened the microwave on the counter behind the bar and set another slice on a piece of paper towel then touched the "Quick Minute" button and shut the door. As soon as the microwave dinged, he pulled out his hot slice of pizza.

Libby groaned, sounding like she was in agony.

"What's the matter?" he said with his mouth full as he grabbed a bottle of Coke and twisted off the cap. "Hey, are you wearing pajamas?"

"Yeah," she said, pressing the back of her hand against her forehead. "All of my jeans are so tight I can hardly get them buttoned. I feel so much better in these clothes because they have an elastic waist." She pointed toward the food in his hand. "That pizza is making me nauseous."

"It is? Why is that? You're not even eating." He heated two pieces this time, pressed them together like a sandwich, and began to devour them.

"Ugh...it's the smell—too strong. All that grease makes me feel like I wanna—"

He tossed the crust into the box, wiped his hands on a piece of paper towel, and grabbed another bottle of Coke. "You need something to drink. A little sugar will make you feel better." Walking toward her, he twisted off the cap and a rush of sweet-smelling aroma hissed from the bottle.

"Yuck, I can't." Grimacing, she pushed his hand away. "Get it away from me."

"Whatever you say," he said and recapped the bottle.

"Cash," she said quietly, "what are we going to do? How are we going to pay our bills?"

"I've been thinking about that," he replied and studied her reaction, anxious to tell her his plans. "It's going to be tough for a while, but we can make it. Financially, I mean."

She lifted her head and stared at him, waiting for him to continue.

"You'll have to go back to school after the kid comes," he said seriously. "We'll work it out with the guidance counselor to make sure you get tutoring until you're ready to return to classes. Thing is, we're going to need a babysitter we can trust but we can't pay for one...so I'm going to get my mom to do it."

Libby frowned. "Are you sure? She just retired. She's not going to like being tied down."

"She'll be in retirement for a year by that time. Besides, my dad plans to keep working for another five years so they don't have any plans to travel anytime soon. I'll talk to her." Cash reached over to the box on the counter and grabbed another slice of pizza. "This is her first grandchild. She'll be excited about the baby once she gets used to the idea. She'll do it to help us."

"What about you?" Libby pulled a clip from her hair and her thick blonde mane tumbled down her arms. "What about college? How can you go if you have a family to support?"

"I got a job today on a construction crew. I'm starting on Monday," Cash replied, feeling confident. "I figure I'll work during the day and go to school at night."

She nervously toyed with the clip as she stared at him. "I worry that it'll be too much for you."

"My parents went through tough times and survived," he stated. "We can, too."

He ate the rest of his pizza slowly and thought about what it would be like to have a child of his own. Scary stuff, he had to admit, but he knew a couple of other guys who'd become a father at a young age and they were handling it just fine.

Libby surprised him by standing up and suddenly putting her arms around him. "No matter what, we're going to let our child know every day that she is *loved*."

He dropped the pizza back in the box and drew her closer, resting his chin on the top of her head. "I'm glad you mentioned that."

"Why?"

Cash drew in a deep breath, unsure of how she would handle his answer. "Well, I understand why you believe God has abandoned you, but I think you should give Him another chance."

She stiffened, warning him that he'd tread upon a touchy subject. "What do you mean by that," she replied, sounding wary.

"Because I want both of us to take our kid to church every Sunday. Get him baptized, too. Maybe send him to a Christian school if we can afford it by the time he's ready to start. We don't want him acting out when he grows up and pulling the same stunts we did."

She pulled back and folded her arms, frowning. "What makes you think shoving all that religion down her throat will guarantee her good behavior? It didn't work for *us*."

"I don't know." He looked into her eyes. "But I do know we have to do the best we can to raise him right, okay?"

She didn't answer. Suddenly, her face began to take on a greenish tinge and she repeatedly swallowed, as though trying to get rid of the saliva filling her mouth.

"Libby, what's wrong? Are you okay?"

She pushed him away, her face taking on a green tinge. "The pizza smell—it's all over you. I've gotta get out of—" Covering her mouth with her hand, she stumbled toward the door.

Cash helplessly watched as she jerked open the door and burst outside, barely in time before she began to throw up.

Chapter Seven

"Libby, *get up* and get ready. We're leaving for church in fifteen minutes!"

Feeling worse than she did the previous night, Libby dragged herself out of bed and slogged her way to the top of the stairs. Her head swam with dizziness and the aroma of fried bacon wafting from the kitchen steadily increased that queasy spot in the pit of her stomach. "I can't go. I'm sick."

Norma stopped at the foot of the stairs and stared up at her. She wore a burgundy suit with matching shoes. In one hand, she gripped her clutch handbag and a pair of short, white gloves. Her other hand rested on the pineapple-shaped newel post. "What's wrong?"

Libby grasped onto the newel post to keep herself upright. "I'm dizzy and I feel like throwing up."

Norma silently stared up at her, creating a tense moment. "You must have the flu that's going around. Go back to bed and get some rest," she replied tersely. "I'll be home later. In the meantime, Delores will bring you some hot tea."

"Okay, thanks, Grandma," Libby said weakly, exceedingly glad to spend the day in her jammies. She turned and stumbled back to bed, sliding under the still warm covers, and went back to sleep.

It took most of the day to get past the nausea and gain her strength back. By afternoon, the hot, salty chicken soup that Delores made for her had settled her stomach so she could sit up and watch television. Norma had instructed Delores to check her temperature, which turned out to be normal.

*   *   *

Libby felt well enough to attend school the next day. She still suffered from nausea in the early morning, but a cold glass of orange juice and a piece of buttered toast with jam helped somewhat. She wore a loose dress and flat sandals for comfort, as most of her jeans no longer fit in the waist. She needed to hold on just a couple more days until school ended. Then she had the entire summer to relax.

School ended on Wednesday with a seventh-period farewell party in the gymnasium and sugary treats baked by the school lunchroom staff. Libby said goodbye to all her friends, promising to meet up with them at Harriet Lake beach on hot days and hang out at the band shell during the free concerts sponsored by the Minneapolis Park Board.

"Give me a call next week," Medley told Libby at the party. "Let me know what happens when you...you know, talk to your dad."

"For sure," Libby said as her stomach churned with apprehension. She was happy about the baby but dreaded the ugly scene that would unfold when she broke the news to her father—and Norma. Since the moment she found out about the baby, she'd purposely avoided thinking about it. "I don't know yet what day he'll be home. He usually doesn't know himself until the last minute."

Cash met her at the party and sat with her in the lunchroom, holding her hand under the table as they chatted with friends. "How's it going today?" He dipped his head close to hers. "Feeling okay?"

Libby took a deep breath. "Yeah, I'm doing a lot better this afternoon. I almost threw up in the washroom this morning."

He gave her a teasing grin and squeezed her hand. "Well, now you've got the whole summer to do pretty much what you want while some of us have to work all week. What do you have planned for tomorrow?"

She sighed. "Sleeping in!"

*   *   *

Cash left the party early and headed straight for the nature center to meet Libby. Except for a few joggers who didn't mind the heat during this portion of the day, the center usually had sparse attendance this late in the afternoon. He wanted to spend some quality time with her because he didn't know when he'd get another chance to see her again now that school was out. His construction job started immediately, plus he had night classes at the university, so for now, they had little opportunity to be together.

Besides, he had a special surprise for her.

He waited at the entrance until he saw her approaching the large gates in white leggings and a peach top. The moment they made eye contact, he smiled and signaled for her to meet him at their usual place in the woods.

He proceeded along the trail to an area where a smaller path branched off from the main one. He leaned against a tree, waiting for her. Moments later, Libby rounded the curve. The moment their gazes connected, she burst into a smile and ran to him.

"Hey," he murmured as she fell into his arms. "I couldn't wait for the party to end today so we could be alone."

She gazed lovingly into his eyes. "Me, too! We can be ourselves here. We don't have to worry about anyone seeing us together."

He kissed her slowly, savoring the moment. With his new job starting tomorrow, he didn't know when they'd get a chance to meet like

70

this again.

"I'm so-o-o glad school is over for this year," Libby said with a sigh as they walked along the trail holding hands. "We did it!"

They hugged each other and laughed.

She punched him in the shoulder. "You're so lucky. You never have to go back there again."

"Oh, I'm lucky, all right." He shot her a wry smile and rubbed the place where she smacked him, pretending it hurt. "Now I get to go to college and work, too, and most likely trade sleeping for study time."

She gave him a mischievous grin. "How would you like to exchange places and have this baby instead?"

He stopped and burst out laughing. "Me? Nope. I'd just as soon shingle a roof on a ninety-degree day than go through *that*." He tilted her face toward his and kissed her lips. "Better you than me, little mama. But just so you know that I care...this is for you." He held up her palm and slipped a ring on her finger. It fitted perfectly.

Libby gasped with surprise as she stared at the tiny diamond solitaire embedded in the yellow-gold promise ring on her finger.

"It's not much—all a college boy can afford—but I'll get you a bigger one someday, a couple of carats if you want," Cash blurted, feeling embarrassed at the microscopic size of the gem.

She looked up, tears spilling from her eyes. "It's beautiful. I don't care what size it is. It's your love that counts."

He pulled her close. "Well, then it's worth a million to me because I think about you all the time. I can't imagine life without you." He closed his fingers over hers and pressed them to his chest. "I'll always love you, Libby. Forever."

Chapter Eight

Thursday, June 1st

"Miss Libby, wake up!"

Libby pried open her eyes to find Delores gently shaking her. "What time is it?" She squinted at her alarm clock and then uttered a groan.

Eight o'clock? Is that all?

The short, dark-haired woman wearing a light green housekeeping uniform bent over her and whispered, "I'm sorry to get you out of bed so early on your first day of summer vacation, but Mrs. Cunningham sent me up here to tell you that your father is home, and he wants to see you."

Delores' words surprised her. *Dad's home? What time did he get in,* Libby wondered as she became fully awake. She would have surely heard his footsteps on the stairs had he arrived in the middle of the night...unless he'd gone straight to the gazebo instead. She hadn't seen him but twice in as many months and had missed him terribly.

Yawning, she sat up in bed and stretched. "Did he see my report card? I think we should celebrate!"

Delores pointed toward a small tray on her dresser. "Senator Cunningham didn't say, but I brought you some orange juice and a cinnamon roll just in case you were hungry."

"Okay, thanks, Delores," Libby replied with an appreciative smile. "Tell him I'll be right down."

Delores left the room, shutting the door behind her. Libby pulled back the covers and slid out of bed, going straight for the juice. The cool, sweet liquid tasted good going down her throat, staving off the queasiness for now. She took a bite of the cinnamon roll and licked a bit of the frosting off her finger then rifled through her dresser for something comfortable to wear. She pulled on a pair of pastel blue cotton knit shorts and a babydoll top in white eyelet, drew a brush through her long hair, and went downstairs to the breakfast room to find her father.

But he wasn't there.

She found him in his office, discussing something with Norma.

"Listen to me," Norma said so loudly that Libby could hear it before she reached the room. "You need to take care of this *now*. Send her to the Caribbean for a procedure and be done with it!"

"I can't take that chance and you know it," Frank shot back heatedly. "If the press found out it would be the end of my career! No, my way is better."

Libby approached the door and hesitated. What were they talking about? The urgency in their voices caused her to pull back. Too late— Frank cleared his throat, indicating he'd heard her footsteps on the oak flooring.

"Hi, Dad," Libby said cautiously as she moved into the doorway. "When—when did you get home?"

The senator sat at his massive mahogany desk, wearing a light blue polo shirt and beige sports slacks, the type of clothes he usually wore on the days he planned to play golf. Even when dressed casually, his tall, lean features and quiet manner projected the confident air of a successful attorney and a powerful dignitary.

The moment Libby entered the room Norma abruptly ceased lecturing the senator. She turned toward Libby, her gray eyes hardening to stone behind her glasses.

The Senator ignored his mother's reaction. Instead, he turned to his daughter and said gently, "Come here, Libby. I want to talk to you."

The calm in his voice sounded forced, tighter controlled than usual and it threw her into an instant panic.

Oh-oh, now what did I do?

Her stomach fluttered as she gingerly stepped into her father's office and approached his desk. "Wh-what do you want to talk about?" Glancing between him and Norma, she sensed something was terribly wrong. "What's going on? Is this about my grades? I got Bs this semester! I'm even passing in algebra!"

The Senator started to answer, but his mother cut him off. "Why don't you tell *us* what's going on with you and that boy you've been chasing around with behind your father's back?"

Libby's jaw dropped in surprise. How did they find out? *Did Medley break her promise and tell one of them?*

Keeping his attention focused on Libby, the Senator said, "Mother, please allow me—"

"You've been seeing that long-haired ruffian, Cash MacKenzie, every day after school and sneaking out of the house at night, too. Don't deny it! We've got proof."

Grandma Norma's accusation left Libby flabbergasted. "What proof?"

Norma's lips pressed into a tight line. "That's none of your business."

Libby turned to her father. "Dad, what is she talking about? Who told you about Cash and me? Did you talk to Medley?"

The senator gave her a quizzical frown. "Medley?" He glanced at his mother as lines of concern etched into his brow. "Is she involved with him as well? I don't recall seeing any information on her."

Realizing her error, Libby shook her head, afraid she'd wrongly implicated her cousin. "No, no, she doesn't have anything to do with Cash or me. I rarely talk to her at school because we don't have any classes together. I just wondered if she'd said anything about me, that's all. Dad," Libby persisted, becoming upset, "what did you do—pay someone to snoop around and follow us?"

"You mean, what tipped us off?" Norma spat. She reached out, opened a side drawer of the desk, and produced the box containing the home pregnancy test. Her eyes narrowed as she slammed it on the desktop. "I found it in the trash bin. You little sneak! I should have known you'd pull a stupid stunt like this. You're nothing but a tramp, Olivia, just like your mother!"

"Don't talk about my mother like that!" Libby turned to her father. "Dad, can we talk—just you and me?"

The senator's face suddenly flushed, as though struggling to keep his temper in check. "Mother, I told you, *I'll* handle this—"

"It didn't take Frank's man long to get the goods on the two of you. He simply followed you and you led him right to the boy," she continued, as though she hadn't heard her son. She grabbed the box and shook it in Libby's face. "Don't you realize what you've done? If word of this gets out, the press will go berserk. It'll ruin your father's career—"

The senator sprang from his chair and towered over her. "Mother, if you will excuse us, I want to speak with my daughter privately."

"Why should I?" She threw her hands upward, her eyes blazing. "This concerns me just as much as it does you. All the sacrifices I've made to put you in Washington and keep you there is in serious jeopardy because of her!"

75

Placing his hands on his hips, he glared at her. "We'll talk about that when I'm finished here. Leave us, please, *now*."

Flustered, his mother stomped out of the room. The senator followed her and shut the door behind her to make sure she complied, but Libby knew her grandmother would never give up that easily. The stubborn, prideful old bag probably stood outside the door, listening in.

Frank turned around and walked slowly toward his desk. A grave frown deepened the lines in his face. "Sit down."

Alone with her father, Libby sat on the edge of her chair, processing the fact that he'd retained a private investigator to trail after her and Cash and give an account of their every movement back to him. Horrified, she worried about what the man had witnessed, but more importantly, what he'd reported to her father.

"Dad, why did you do that?" She swallowed hard, preventing angry tears from surfacing. "How long have you been violating my privacy by paying someone to spy on me?"

The senator folded his hands in front of him on the desk, giving her the feeling that confronting her made him extremely uncomfortable. Except for a small spot of perspiration on the soft gray lining his temple, however, he kept his emotions under control.

"The man I used is someone I trust," he said, evading her question. "Brady's the one I call upon whenever I'm dealing with a sensitive matter." He looked into her eyes. "I understand you've been seeing that young man almost every day and sometimes at night. I need to know. Are you..." he blinked, "pregnant?"

"Yes, *I am*, but you already know that. I'm four and a half months along," Libby replied defiantly and frowned at him, expecting to hear that she'd once again alienated herself from God by her actions. But the lecture didn't come.

Instead, pain and disappointment flickered across her father's face. His brief reaction stunned her, making her suddenly realize how deeply she'd hurt him. She'd never seen him react that way before—the look of utter helplessness and grief—as though he'd lost someone dear to him. That awful sense of guilt pressed upon her once again, crushing her spirit.

"I'm sorry, Dad," she said as she bowed her head and began sobbing like a child. "I mean it. I know I've let you down, but I never meant to hurt you. It's just that—"

"No, *I'm* the one who is sorry." He cleared his throat, struggling to speak. "I've let *you* down, honey. I've neglected you for years and I regret what my failure as a father has done to you. Your grandmother did the best she could to raise you in my place, but she's no substitute for the mother you should have had."

He stood up and stretched out his arms. Libby bolted around the desk and hugged him tightly, holding nothing back. "Dad, I miss you so much," she said through her sobs. "I realize your job is important and that you don't have a lot of control over your schedule, but it's so difficult being alone all of the time. I've spent most of my life waiting for you to come home so we could be together like a real family."

"I know, honey. It's been rough on you and I'm sorry for that," he whispered as he rested his cheek on the top of her head and patted her hair. "You need a caring mother to talk to about sensitive issues. I should have agreed to let Barbara take you under her wing. If I had, things would have turned out differently."

She looked up. "But now *I'm* going to be a mother and I'm determined to make sure my baby is never alone," she announced with a loud sniffle. "Cash and I both intend to show her unconditional love."

His troubled expression quickly turned gravely serious. "Cash MacKenzie is not a part of your life any longer."

"Yes, he is," Libby argued, "we're going to get married." She held up her hand and showed him the promise ring. "He gave this to me yesterday!"

The senator dismissed the ring with a shake of his head. "You're *too* young and immature to get married. Or to raise a child. So is he." He let out a terse sigh. "That would be a worse mistake than what we're dealing with now."

"That's not true, Dad," Libby argued. "We understand it's not going to be easy at first, but we're committed to each other. Things are going to work out. You'll see."

"Listen to me!" He grasped her by the arms and silenced her with a stern shake. "I love you too much to let you ruin your life over a boy who's not worthy of you. He took advantage of you and got you into this mess, but that part of your life is over. I'm going to help you rectify the situation—from today forward—and we're never looking back."

The decisive tone of his reply alarmed her. "What do you mean by that?"

Still grasping her by the arms, he gently pressed her down onto her chair and stood over her. "There will be no marriage. The child will be placed for adoption."

Libby gasped in horror. "No! No, I won't do that! I won't give up Cash and my baby!"

His voice became calm again, devoid of emotion, but the pain of his decision was reflected in his eyes. "Libby, it's the only way you're going to get your life back on track. Don't you understand? You've made a bad mistake, but you can start over. Once the baby is placed in a new home and our situation goes back to normal, you can start fresh at another private school, make new friends, and build the great life I've always envisioned for you."

"No! I don't want your version of a great life." Libby began to cry again but from anger this time. "I've already got everything I've ever wanted. I have Cash and our baby!"

He took a deep breath and placed a hand on her shoulder. "I know you're upset right now, but one day you'll understand. At this point in your life, adoption is the best decision for both you and the child."

"No! No! I won't do it!" she shrieked. "I don't care what you say. I'll never give up my baby!"

Shoving his hand away, she sprang from the chair and ran out of the room, passing her grandmother on her way out.

Chapter Nine

Cash came home from his first day of construction work exhausted, sweaty, and covered with grime. His mother, a short, slender woman with curly salt-and-pepper hair held a stack of plates in her hands, setting the table as he walked through the kitchen door. Barney, Cash's Irish setter, trotted into the kitchen, wagging his long, furry tail.

"Hey, Mom, dinner really smells good," Cash said and breathed in the pungent aroma of roast beef. He reached down and gave the dog an affectionate pat. Then he opened a cupboard door and pulled out an open bag of Oreos. "I'm starving."

"The roast is coming out of the oven in five minutes. All I have left to do is make the gravy. Your father should be home by the time you get out of the shower and then we'll eat," Maggie told him as she snatched the bag out of his hand and put it back in the cupboard. "Hurry along and get cleaned up. You know your father hates to wait for his dinner."

Cash crammed two cookies into his mouth, pulled his filthy T-shirt over his head, and headed upstairs to his room to jump into the shower with Barney following on his heels. The thought of stuffing himself with roast, potatoes and his mother's fantastic gravy made his stomach growl. He couldn't wait to dig in!

Twenty minutes later, as he emerged from the upstairs bathroom, he heard male voices coming from the living room and wondered if his older sisters, Sherry and Leanne had shown up with their boyfriends. Both were students at St. Thomas University and lived on campus, but that didn't stop them from dropping in for a home-cooked meal and dessert, especially if they knew their mother was preparing a family favorite like roast beef.

"My son will be down in a minute," he heard Maggie speak stiffly to someone.

"I'm coming, Ma," Cash hollered as he bounded down the stairs in a fresh pair of jeans and a white T-shirt. "Who's here—"

The words died on his lips the moment he entered the living room and saw his mother sitting on the arm of the sofa, wearing a deep frown, her hard stare warning him that something was terribly amiss. His father sat on the sofa with his arm around Maggie, silently assessing the situation. Barney crouched on the floor next to his parents, a ridge of hair standing up along his spine.

Two men in black suits stood in the middle of the room, staring at him expectantly.

The hair on the back of his neck began to prickle. *Who died?*

He stared at his parents in puzzlement. "What's going on?" He gestured toward *the suits*. "Who's this?"

The tallest one, a straight-faced individual with short, meticulously combed hair as dark as his attire stepped forward. "Are you Cash Mackenzie?"

"Yeah," he answered warily. "Who are you and what do you want?"

"I'm Mr. Brown and my associate is Mr. Graves. We're here on behalf of Senator Cunningham to deliver a message to you." The man's voice held no emotion, yet the effect came across as deadly serious.

Cash's heart began to slam in his chest. He glanced at his parents. Maggie and Ray MacKenzie remained motionless, waiting for him to speak.

"What is this about?" he demanded placing his hands on his hips.

Graves, the shorter, stocky man with wavy red hair stepped forward. "You've been seeing Senator Cunningham's daughter against his wishes." The man pierced Cash with his cold, detached gaze. "As of this moment, your relationship with her *no longer exists.*"

Cash moved closer, getting in the man's face. Barney growled. "That's for Libby to decide."

The dark-haired man, Mr. Brown, joined his companion, and together, they faced-off with Cash.

"Senator Cunningham was explicit in his instructions to us. This is not a request," Mr. Brown said in a steel-soft voice. "Your relationship with his daughter, Olivia, is hereby terminated and you're never to contact her again. Do you understand?"

Maggie sprang from the arm of the sofa. "What's going on here?" She turned to Cash. "How did you get involved with Senator Cunningham's daughter and why have you been seeing her if her father doesn't approve?"

Cash glanced at Maggie and tried to remain calm, but he couldn't contain his anger at such high-handed treatment at the hands of the senator's paid goons. "We met at school, and I've been seeing her for a while. I planned to tell you about her this weekend after I heard from her, but—" He gave their unwanted visitors a pointed stare. "It looks like her old man beat me to it."

Maggie looked directly at Mr. Brown and dramatically waved her hand, demonstrating her disapproval of the way the Senator had handled the situation. "Look, Mr. Brown, I'm sure my son didn't mean any harm by being attentive to Senator Cunningham's daughter. He's a good kid.

He gets excellent grades and has lettered in sports. You can't stop teenagers from being friends when they attend the same school, so what's the problem? And why didn't the Senator contact us directly if he didn't approve of their friendship? We could have discussed the issue parent-to-parent."

"Senator Cunningham doesn't mean any disrespect, ma'am," Mr. Graves said politely, "but he's a very busy man who prefers to handle his personal business with utmost privacy. A trip to your house would not be in his best interests."

"You mean he wants to keep this out of the press." Maggie's hazel eyes narrowed as she glanced between her son and Mr. Brown. "So, in other words, there's more to this story than just a simple boy-girl crush, isn't there? What else is going on that we should know about?"

Sweat began to collect on the back of Cash's neck. This was definitely *not* the way he wanted his mother to find out about Libby! "Ah...Libby and I—"

"Ma'am," Mr. Brown said, cutting in, "since your son, here, obviously didn't want you to know about his midnight escapades with Ms. Cunningham in the guest house on the senator's property, I'll cut to the chase and do it for him. Mr. MacKenzie has been literally sneaking around behind the senator's back with his sixteen-year-old daughter for the last five months and now unfortunately the girl is pregnant."

Maggie's loud gasp forced him to stop talking.

"The senator is quite protective of her," Mr. Brown said, continuing, "and as a result, he's taking this matter very seriously. He has sent us here to inform you that his daughter no longer wishes to see your son."

"That's a lie!" Cash stepped between his mother and the man. "The last time I saw Libby, everything was great between us. She couldn't wait to see me again!"

"Any attempt to contact her—ever—will be construed as harassment," Mr. Brown continued in a warning tone, "and the senator will press charges against you on her behalf."

Barney began to bark, the ridge on his back becoming sharper. Ray reached out and gently wrapped his fingers around the dog's collar to restrain him.

An eerie silence fell over the group. Maggie's face blanched as her mouth slowly dropped open wide enough to swallow an entire courtroom. "Oh. Dear. God, she said slowly as she turned to Cash. "This girl is pregnant? What were you thinking? She's only sixteen!"

"Ma," Cash said in a rush, "I know it sounds bad, and I'm sorry I didn't tell you about her before, but it's not what you think. Libby and I are in love, and we want to get married. The baby...I...it was a mistake, but I intend to make it right."

Color returned to Maggie's face in a rush of frustration. "You call getting a teenage girl pregnant out of wedlock a mere *mistake*? That is not how I raised you, Cash MacKenzie! You went to a good Christian school for six years and we've tried to instill biblical values in you since you were born. You know better!"

"Ma, I'm sorry," Cash sputtered, knowing it sounded lame, but he couldn't think of anything else to say. "I didn't mean for things to turn out this way."

His father suddenly stood at his side. "Look, Mr. Brown, this is the first time we've heard about Cash's involvement with the senator's daughter, and we have no proof of anything you're claiming. Can you say without a doubt that the child she's carrying is his?"

Heat rose up the back of Cash's neck. "*Dad—*"

Ray MacKenzie held up his hand to silence his son. "Hold on. Let me finish." He turned back to Mr. Brown. "There's no way we're simply going to take your word for it. After the baby is born, we'll request a paternity test and if my son is the father, I guarantee you he'll take care of his obligations to his child. In the meantime, I do believe the senator owes me a personal phone call to discuss the issue and I would appreciate it if you would relay that message back to him."

"I will," Mr. Brown said as he nodded at Ray, "but it won't be necessary for the boy to establish paternity. The senator isn't interested in holding him financially responsible. He simply wants your son to leave his daughter alone."

"Until Libby tells me herself that she doesn't want to see me any longer," Cash said, getting angry again, "I'm not giving her up. I love her and I have the right to be involved in my child's life!"

Mr. Brown stared hard at Cash. "You *will* respect the senator's wishes or there'll be consequences!"

"Yes, sir," Maggie said, interrupting the exchange. "Cash understands that the senator is in a difficult position and is making decisions based on what's best for his family. We all do. He won't cause the senator—or his daughter—any more problems."

"Thank you," Mr. Brown said politely. "Senator Cunningham also requests confidentiality on the issue of the child until he and his daughter decide on her future plans."

After acknowledging Ray MacKenzie's nod of approval, the two men thanked him and Maggie for their understanding of the matter and walked to the front entrance. At the door, Mr. Brown paused. "I'll relay your message to the senator, Mr. MacKenzie."

After they left, no one spoke for a few moments. Cash leaned against the wall with his arms folded, staring at the floor in a daze, turning over in his mind one statement that Mr. Brown made.

His daughter no longer wishes to see your son...

Desperation and helplessness washed over him. He clenched his fists. *It's a lie!*

How did Cunningham find out? Libby would never have approached him alone. She'd made it clear she wanted Cash by her side when she told her father about the baby. Did someone else tell him? At this point, it didn't matter, but the fact remained that he couldn't see Libby—or his child without getting himself into serious trouble. The senator's aides had made that perfectly clear. Still, he had to see her one more time and hear it from her, regardless of the outcome. He couldn't let her go until he knew for sure.

"Well, well…" Maggie said dryly, breaking the silence, "that was a pleasant start to the weekend." She turned to Cash. "I can't believe we had to hear about it from someone else! You should have come to us about this right away instead of keeping us in the dark. How could you do this to us?"

"Ma, I didn't do it deliberately to hurt you." Cash let out a deep sigh. "Besides, I'm the one who's hurting right now. Can't you see that?"

"No," Maggie snapped as she blinked back angry tears. "All I see is the shame you've caused this family. You snuck around with a girl you had no business pursuing, did things you should be ashamed of and now she's in trouble." She shook her finger at him. "And so are you!"

"I didn't keep our relationship a secret to deceive you," Cash argued in desperation to make her understand his side of the story. "I did it to protect her. If her father found out about us—"

"He'd have stopped all of the nonsense going on between you two before you got her pregnant!" She pulled a Kleenex from a box on the coffee table and dabbed her nose. "You owe your father and me an apology for putting us through this!"

Cash hung his head with contrition. "I never thought it would come to this. Like I said, I never meant to hurt you." He let out a tense sigh. "But in the end, I guess I managed to hurt everyone, didn't I?"

Ray ran a hand through his thick gray hair. "Maggie, please calm down. Can't you see the boy is distraught? This is as difficult for him as it is for us. He's got a lot to process right now."

She whirled around. "He's distraught? What about me? I'm about to be a grandmother for the first time to an illegitimate child I'll probably never even get to hold!"

Ray put his arms around Maggie and gently patted her back, trying to comfort her. "I know this isn't how you'd envisioned getting your first grandchild, but unfortunately, we don't have any control over the situation. It is what it is. So, come on, let's put it in God's hands and eat dinner. Life must go on."

"Oh, for crying out loud. I forgot all about dinner sitting on the table." Maggie pulled away, fraught with frustration. "The roast is cold by now. The coleslaw is wilted—"

"It'll be just fine, Mags," Ray said gently. "We can warm up the beef in the microwave."

Maggie went into the kitchen to salvage the meal, but Cash held back. Considering what he'd just learned, he didn't care now whether he ate or not. "I suppose you're disappointed in me, too," he said to his father. "A pretty girl captures my heart, and all of my upbringing goes out the window."

Ray looked him squarely in the eye. "What you did was wrong, but I'm not going to criticize you for it. I was young once. I did a few things I'm not proud of as well. I just hope this tragedy has taught you a good lesson. The consequences of your actions can cause permanent damage to other lives because some mistakes can never be fixed."

"Yeah," Cash said slowly, "like falling in love with a girl who *supposedly* doesn't want anything to do with me anymore."

Ray put his broad palm on Cash's shoulder. "Don't worry son. We'll get through this."

Much to Cash's chagrin, that's exactly what he'd promised Libby. His heart sank at the realization that he'd let her down. He had to see her one more time to tell her how sorry he was and promise her that one day they'd be together again. He just had to! He couldn't let her think he didn't care.

The trouble was, he had no idea how to do that without getting them both in trouble. The last thing he wanted to do was cause more problems for Libby.

I'll find a way, he thought desperately. *I have to. We can't end things like this.*

Their future happiness depended on it.

Chapter Ten

Libby stood inside the front porch of her Aunt Barbara's three-story Victorian home and leaned on the doorbell. She desperately needed to see Medley. If she could convince Medley to go along with her plan, then perhaps together they could sway Barbara and Bob as well. She needed as much support from her extended family as she could muster!

Cupping her hands around her eyes to shield them from the bright June sun, she peered through the long, oval glass of the front door, straining to see if she could spot anyone inside the Grant residence. To her dismay, the foyer stood empty.

She tried the door handle but found it locked. She rang the bell again and waited, but no one appeared in the foyer. Discouraged, she let out a defeated sigh. Where were they? Hopefully, they'd be home soon. Determined to wait for them, she shut the screen door and turned away, deciding to roll her bike around to the rear of the house and collapse into the hammock under the trees until they arrived. The long ride in the heat of the day had taken its toll on her, causing her to crave a refreshing gulp of cold water from the garden hose to cool down and a place to take a nap.

Just as she turned to go, a movement inside the house caught her eye. She spun around as Barbara turned the dead bolt lock and swung open the front door. Like Medley, her aunt was of medium height with dark brown hair and hazel eyes. In her mid-forties, Barbara wore her shoulder-length hair in spiral curls and favored gold hoop earrings. Today she wore a pair of capri pants in cream and a loose-fitting tunic top in lavender with three-quarter sleeves.

"Libby! How nice to see you. I'm sorry it took me so long to let you in," she said opening the screen door to let Libby inside. A pair of thin gold bracelets jangled on her wrist as she gestured for Libby to enter the house. "You caught me on the telephone. Come in."

Libby walked into a narrow foyer with oak flooring and wide, dark-stained woodwork. "Is Medley home?"

Barbara closed the front door and followed her into the house, her bare feet padding softly on the wood flooring. "No, she's in Chicago for three days. Didn't she tell you about her trip? She went with a group from her art class on a museum tour. Someone in her class cancelled at the last minute and she was offered the slot. It was a last-minute arrangement so perhaps she planned to call you from the hotel. Did you girls have something special planned for today?"

"No, I just stopped by to talk." Libby's disappointment swelled. Now what would she do? She'd counted on Medley's help!

"Joe is at a conference in Kansas City," Barbara said, "so I've got the entire weekend to myself. I've been wandering around the house all afternoon, wondering what to do." She led the way through the foyer into a living room furnished with overstuffed black furniture and a room-sized rug in red with a black diamond pattern. "Sit down. Make yourself comfortable," she said as she plucked a couple of stray magazines off the sofa. "Would you like something to drink? You look a little flushed."

Exhausted and sick to her stomach from the heat, Libby collapsed onto the soft sofa and exhaled deeply, brushing her hair from her sweaty forehead. "Yes, I'd like some water, please. I'm so hot I'm dizzy."

Barbara went into the kitchen and returned a couple of minutes later with two tumblers of ice water garnished with a slice of fresh lemon and a small plate of iced ginger snap cookies. "Here," she said as she handed a glass to Libby, "this should hit the spot."

Barbara placed the cookies on the coffee table and sat in an armchair, tucking her legs underneath her. "Is everything all right with Frank? I heard he's back home for a day or so, but then he's returning to Washington."

Libby drank the entire glass of water and set the tumbler on a wrought iron coffee table with a glass top. She fell back against a pair of large sofa pillows, fighting the urge to cry. "He came back because of me."

Barbara swallowed a sip of water and frowned. "Why? What became so urgent that it caused him to drop everything and fly home?"

Her aunt's lack of information surprised her. Apparently, her father didn't tell his sister everything that went on in his family life. However, knowing she had no one else to turn to, Libby decided to confide in Barbara, anyway. "Grandma called him and told him I was pregnant."

Barbara froze; her eyes widening with shock at the news. "You're..." She stared at Libby, holding the tumbler of ice water frozen in mid-air. "Is it the boy you've been meeting at Sandhill Nature Center every afternoon? The handsome one with black hair? Is he the father?"

Libby scrambled to a sitting position, hugging a large red accent pillow. "How did you know that Cash and I met at the nature center?"

"I've been doing volunteer administration work at the interpretive center three days a week for a few months now," Barbara replied as she set her glass down. "The window next to my desk faces the front entrance."

Libby sat up straight, swallowing hard at Barbara's confession. "Did you tell my father about us?"

91

Barbara shook her head. "Knowing how strict he is with you I probably should have but no—I never said a word about it to anyone. I figured it was your business who you spent time with after school."

"Thank you for not telling anyone—especially Grandma."

Drawing in a tense breath, Barbara stared at the floor with a deep frown as though she found the situation profoundly sad. "You always looked so happy when you were with him. You were utterly radiant. I wanted to talk to you about this boy and find out more about the situation because I knew you needed guidance, but at the same time, if Frank found out about my involvement, he'd simply tell me not to interfere." Her steely tone of voice suggested that she resented her brother for deliberately shutting her out of his issues with his teenage daughter.

"Dad says I have to place the baby for adoption and go on with my life. He said I was too young and immature for such a heavy responsibility and that Cash was too. I'm not allowed to see him anymore." Libby slid to the edge of the sofa hugging the pillow tightly to her chest. "Auntie Barbara, I don't want to give up my baby. Other girls my age have had babies and raised them without any problem. I can do it, too. I know I can, but I don't have to go through it by myself. I can marry Cash and have the happy, loving family I've never had!"

Her aunt moved to the sofa and sat next to her.

"Oh, honey, I don't know what to say about that except that I love you very much and I'm sorry you're going through this." Barbara pulled the pillow from Libby's hands and held her close. "Marriage at your age would only compound your problems so I understand why Frank is against it. That said, I don't think it's right to separate you from your child! Frank is wrong about that, but if he's adamant about the adoption, I doubt that I can change his mind." She smiled lovingly. "I'll talk to him, though, if you want me to."

"Yes, I do! Thank you." Libby looked up, gazing into Barbara's eyes. "May I stay here with you and Uncle Bob? If I lived with you, the press wouldn't pay attention to me, and I wouldn't be an embarrassment to Dad. I won't cause you any trouble, I promise! I don't ever want to go home again." Her eyes filled with tears. "They don't want me, anyway."

The concern in Barbara's eyes turned to shock at Libby's confession. "Of course they do! Frank and Norma love you."

Libby shook her head. "Grandma is really mad. She said that my actions may have jeopardized Dad's career. He wants me to go to a Christian home for unwed mothers until I have the baby instead of living at home. He's probably ashamed of me. I don't want to go, but I know that's what he and Grandma expect." A tear dropped from her eye. "They're getting rid of me because I'm a troublemaker!"

Her aunt gave her a deep hug. "You're not a troublemaker, Libby. I'm sure they just want the best care for you and the baby."

"I asked Dad to forgive me, and he did, but he's still sending me away and Grandma won't even talk to me." Libby looked down at her hands. "I feel so alone."

"Darling, you're not alone," Barbara said as she cradled Libby's face in her palms. "I'll always be here for you."

She picked up the living room extension and punched in a number, the musical tones of the keypad forming a strange tune. After a few moments, she hung up. "That's odd. He's not answering his mobile phone." She began punching in another number. "I'll try the gazebo."

Frank's private line in the gazebo rang continuously as well.

"Rats, he's not in the gazebo, either." She sighed and punched in a third number. "I'll try the house." After a couple of rings, Barbara gave Libby a 'thumbs up,' indicating that someone had answered it.

"Frank, it's Barb. I'm glad I caught you before you left for Washington. I'm calling about Libby," Barbara said in a serious tone. "Yes, she's here with me. We've been having a heart-to-heart discussion about a few things. She told me about her pregnancy and your decision to send her to a private home—"

Libby couldn't hear her father's voice but knew from Barbara's grave expression that he had plenty to say.

"Yes, Frank," Barbara said unhappily, "I understand all that, but why couldn't she stay here with us? She shouldn't be alone at a time like this. She needs her family."

Libby chewed on a fingernail and tried to guess her father's side of the conversation by watching Barbara's expressions.

"Yes, yes," Barbara said, gesturing with her free hand as she spoke, "I'll find out what her classes are and next fall I'll tutor her until she's ready to return to high school."

Libby clasped her hands tightly, hoping against hope that her aunt could talk her father into agreeing with their plan. Barbara, a former teacher, occasionally did private tutoring during the school year, making her the perfect person for such a task.

"Of course, I'll keep her out of the public eye," Barbara said. "You know you can count on me. I'll even take the girls up to the cabin for the summer if that's what you want. No one in Alden Falls knows I'm your sister." She reclined into a relaxed position. "No, no, you don't have to pay me for her room and board. I'm happy to have her."

Libby grabbed a cookie and nibbled on the sweet, chewy treat covered with vanilla frosting. Just as she began to relax, believing the situation was turning in her favor, Barbara suddenly stopped talking. The enthusiastic expression in her eyes turned into a cold, stone-like stare.

Libby sat on the edge of the sofa, anxiously wondering what had happened to change the course of the conversation so abruptly. Her aunt's icy demeanor usually only surfaced when talking to Grandma Norma...

"*Why*." The word came out of Barbara sounding more like a demand than a question. "Look, I understand what's at stake politically, but why must she be caught up in the middle of it? Let's get real here. She's become an unfortunate casualty of his political career rather than a hindrance to it. Perhaps if she'd been given the nurturing she needed in the first place, she wouldn't be in this predicament." Barbara stood and began pacing a small area, holding the base of the red Trimline phone with one hand and pressing the handset to her ear with the other. "Of course, I realize how much you've sacrificed," she said, her voice growing louder and more emotional as the conversation continued, "but this has nothing to do with *you*." After a few more tense words, she stopped pacing and closed her eyes, as if struggling to maintain her temper. "Put Frank on the phone again."

Please, God, Libby prayed, *let me stay here...*

"Frank, I'm only trying to show her some kindness and understanding. This situation is just as difficult for her as it is for you. You've got to listen to reason—"

Her father said something to Barbara that made the woman's face flush with anger.

"Fine." Barbara's nostrils flared—something that only happened when she became extremely upset. "I'll bring her home, but not until tomorrow. She's spending the night here."

Barbara jammed the handset against the base and dropped the set onto the end table with a loud thump. "I'm sorry, Libby." She gave a loud, exasperated sigh. "Unknown to me, Mother was monitoring the conversation on an extension. I almost had Frank convinced, but when he started to see things my way she broke in and turned him against the idea."

"It's not fair," Libby cried and fell back against the pillows. "I don't want to leave here. This is the only place I feel like I belong. If I can't stay here, then I'm going to run away!"

"No, you're not, young lady," Barbara said in a firm but gentle voice, taking her hand. "You're going to do what's best for your baby. If you love your baby and you want to do what's best for the child, you'll put your personal feelings aside and do what's right instead."

Angry over her own unhappy past, Libby glared at her aunt. "Why didn't anyone do that for me?"

"I don't know." Barbara collapsed onto the sofa again and let out a deep sigh of frustration. "After your mother died, everything changed. Frank loved Elizabeth so much that he nearly went crazy when he lost her. He buried himself in his work to get his mind off his grief and left you with Mother, thinking she'd step in as your surrogate parent. He's always been so absorbed with his life in Washington that he's probably never realized until it was too late that you had virtually *no* parent in your life."

Libby swallowed the rest of her cookie and washed it down with ice-cold lemon water. Since her aunt didn't mind answering questions, she had one more for the woman, one that had been plaguing her most of her life. "Auntie Barbara, why doesn't God like me?"

Barbara looked alarmed. "Of course, He likes you. He loves you more than you know."

"Then why doesn't He answer my prayers? Every time I ask Him for help, the situation turns into a disaster instead."

Barbara leaned forward, resting her hands on her knees. "Sometimes it's difficult to understand why things happen the way they do, but the Bible tells us that God's ways are not our ways, and we must simply trust that He knows what's best for us."

"Yeah, but how does losing my mom to a brain aneurysm and living my life as an orphan qualify as good things for me?"

"I can't answer that specifically, dear," Barbara replied softly, "but I do know that God uses all things for our good. Maybe someday you'll gain a better understanding of why you went through so much."

Libby folded her arms. "That doesn't help me right now."

Barbara took one of Libby's hands in hers. "No, but the unhappiness in your past is no reason to live today with your chin hanging down to your toes. You're young and you have your whole life ahead of you. I guarantee you'll get through this and come out stronger on the other side. You can't change the situation, but you can change your attitude. So..." Barbara stood up and pulled Libby to her feet. "Let's go out and get something to eat, have ice cream for dessert then take in a funny movie. Okay?"

Libby smiled through her sadness and nodded her agreement; grateful her aunt understood that her last night of freedom would be the most fun she would undoubtedly experience in a long time.

*   *   *

The next morning Barbara drove Libby home. Upon arrival, they found the house locked. Two black suitcases sat on the front steps with an envelope taped to the handle of the largest one in Grandma Norma's handwriting. Inside they found a note with instructions to wait for a car that would arrive at eleven-thirty to take Libby to her new residence and a small stack of cash for the driver's gratuity. No heartfelt words of goodbye from her grandma or her dad; no instructions to call to let them know she'd arrived safely—nothing but impersonal words on a plain piece of paper.

Barbara expressed her share of outrage by getting the spare key to the house from a secret compartment under the birdbath, unlocking the front door, and promptly calling Frank's mobile phone to give him a piece of her mind.

In the meantime, Libby ran upstairs to her room and stuffed an overnight bag with as many cosmetics and personal items as she could to take with her. She dug underneath the underwear in her top dresser drawer and pulled out the black velvet box containing her promise ring from Cash. She'd tried to call him several times from Barbara's house, but no one answered, leaving her frustrated and even more desperate to

97

talk to him. She shoved the box into her pocket and lugged her bag downstairs.

By the time she reached the receiving hall, an area at the front door with dark woodwork and cream-colored walls, Barbara had finished her telephone call and sat at the kitchen table, drinking a glass of Diet Pepsi.

"Your father is with the Secret Service on his way to the airport. He says he didn't know the house would be empty when we arrived and apologizes for no one being here to see you off."

"Really?" Libby walked into the kitchen and folded her arms as she leaned against the marble countertop of the cooking island. "Why didn't he explain that to me himself?"

"He didn't expect to leave so early, but something has come up and he needs to get back to Washington immediately. He didn't talk long because he was expecting an important call. He sends his regrets and says for you to call him tonight."

Though her aunt tried to sound neutral, the lack of emotion in her voice and the intensity in her eyes suggested that Barbara had all she could do to conceal her disapproval of Frank's continued failure to balance his priorities adequately.

"It's okay," Libby said truthfully. "I'd rather be with you, anyway."

Barbara smiled ruefully and started to say something but stopped abruptly when they heard a car pull into the driveway. Outside they found a black limousine with its motor running. A liveried chauffeur stood at the front door. "I'm here to pick up Miss Olivia Cunningham and take her to the E. Peterson residence in Barna, Minnesota."

Libby stepped forward. "I'm Olivia Cunningham."

"All right, Miss," he said with a smile and a nod. He gestured toward the suitcases. "Are these all of the bags you're taking with you?"

"Yes," Barbara said and took Libby's large overnight bag from her. "Take this one, too."

They watched as the man loaded the suitcases into the trunk of the vehicle. When he finished, he opened the car door for Libby to board.

Before Libby crawled inside, she turned to her aunt for one last conversation. "Thank you, Auntie Barbara, for all you've done for me. I'm so glad you allowed me to stay overnight. You don't know how much it means to me to know that you care. Say goodbye to Medley for me, and Uncle Bob, too. I'll miss you all." Though she tried to be strong, her eyes filled with tears.

"Here," Barbara said thickly and handed her a folded wad of bills. "Your father asked me to give you this." Then she pulled a pocket-sized New Testament from her blazer and a hundred-dollar bill. "This is from me."

She bent forward and kissed Libby on the cheek. "Take care, honey. I'll miss you, too. I love you."

Libby swallowed hard. "I love you, too."

Libby climbed into the limousine and sniffled as she wiped tears from her cheeks with the backs of her hands. She'd never heard of Barna, Minnesota much less how far it was from the Twin Cities. The thought of leaving her friends and the Grants made her sad. She waved at Barbara from the window, noticing how unhappy and defeated her aunt looked standing alone in the driveway trying to keep herself together.

Within a few minutes, the limousine turned onto the freeway and headed north. As the city flew by and the landscape began to change from houses, shopping centers, and factories, into rolling fields and thick, green forests, Libby's thoughts turned to Cash.

For the last two days, she'd avoided thinking about him, holding back all emotion until she could reach him by phone. She wanted to hear his voice once again before giving him the bad news, but she never got the chance because either the MacKenzies had abruptly left town or their phone had been unplugged. It was discouraging, but until she could get a hold of Cash, she had no way of knowing what had caused him to be unavailable.

In the quiet of her seating compartment, thoughts of losing him forever began to overwhelm her heart. In her mind, she saw the thick black hair that framed his lean, tanned face and neck, his generous smile and his brown eyes piercing hers with tenderness and love. She thought of their last meeting at Sandhill Nature Center and opened her hand, cherishing the black velvet ring box nestled in the center of her palm.

At the time, spending eternity with him had seemed so exciting, so inevitable, but now...

Of all the sad times in her life—enduring Christmas without her father, the special events at school that she'd attended with no one to cheer her on, the disappointment of being alone on birthdays and school holidays—she'd never experienced this much loneliness or felt so empty. Since they met, Cash had been her lifeline. He was the only reason she believed she could have the happiness that others took for granted. For her, happiness had always seemed to be an arm's length away.

And now, he'd slipped away, too.

"He said he'd always love me..." she whispered through her tears. "I have to believe that someday he'll come back to me or else I can't go on."

At this point, though, *someday* seemed like a long way off.

So did her chance at happiness.

Part Two

A new direction…

Barna, Minnesota

Chapter Eleven

Friday, June 2nd

Libby's first impression of her new home didn't do much to inspire confidence in her. Barna, Minnesota, population thirty-five, consisted of a gas station, a church, and a small, cinder block building called Smokey's Bar and Grill with apartments on the second floor. Instead of stopping, the limousine flew past the center of town in the blink of an eye. A mile or so down the road they encountered a two-story, Victorian farmhouse with a wraparound porch and detached garage, a large red barn, and several smaller buildings. The limousine slowed at the farmhouse and turned onto the long driveway.

As the car rolled along the sandy lane, Libby stared out the window in dismay. What were they doing here? This couldn't be her home for the next five months. This place looked like something straight out of an old movie! She knocked on the partition separating her from the chauffeur.

"May I help you?" he inquired over the intercom.

"What are we doing here? I thought you were taking me to a private facility."

"This is it," he said, sounding somewhat confused by her question and promptly checked his clipboard. "My orders from Mrs. Cunningham are to deliver you to Elsie Peterson at the Peterson farm in

Barna. Is there a problem?"

Libby blinked in disbelief as she slowly took in the simplicity and remoteness of her surroundings. Ever since her father had broached the subject, she'd envisioned the home to look more like a vacation resort, complete with a pool, restaurant, and rooms with balconies. Did he have any idea what this place was actually like?

Yes, there's a problem, she thought petulantly. *I'm not Rebecca of Sunnybrook Farm. I'm a city girl. I'll never fit in here and I want to go back home! Now!*

"Um, no," she answered, slightly dazed at the truth of her fate. "Thank you."

Now what do I do?

From the corner of her eye, she saw the wooden screen door of the farmhouse fly open and a husky woman in her forties appeared wearing jean shorts and a white boat-necked shirt with red stripes, Reeboks, and ankle socks. The woman's thick brown locks were twisted into a long braid down her back. Curly wisps of stray hair framed her round, tanned face, accentuating her sharp blue eyes. She bounded down the steps and walked quickly to the car. Without waiting for the chauffeur to open Libby's door, she jerked it open. "Hello, there!" She called as she gestured for Libby to come out.

The trouble was, Libby didn't want to come out. She didn't want to spend one more minute in this forgotten place...

The woman bent forward and looked inside the spacious compartment. "You must be Olivia Cunningham," she said with a wide toothy smile. She shoved her hand through the doorway. "I'm Elsie Peterson. Welcome to the Peterson farm."

Libby took her hand, thinking they were going to exchange a friendly shake, but Elsie firmly grabbed hold of her and pulled her out of the vehicle. Once Libby's heeled sandals hit the dirt, she grabbed onto the top of the car door to steady herself. Glancing around she saw a lot of towering trees and odd buildings. Her nostrils drew in an array of pungent aromas, some of which were wafting from the house—like the aroma of freshly baked peach pie.

"You're just in time for dessert," Elsie said in a bold, but friendly voice. "The girls are setting the table so come on into the house and meet your roommates. We'll do introductions and have some pie with whipped cream."

By that time, the chauffeur had begun unloading Libby's bags and setting them on the front sidewalk. Elsie grabbed Libby once again by the hand, literally pulling her toward the house. "Thank you, sir. Just leave the bags right here. We'll take it from here," she said to the chauffeur and then turned to Libby. "Don't be shy now. You're going to get along fine with the other girls. After dessert, we'll bring your bags into the house and get you set up in your room."

Libby glanced back at her suitcases. "Are you sure we should just leave them like that on the sidewalk?"

"Why not? Nobody's going to steal them." Elsie chuckled, embarrassing Libby with her hearty amusement. "Ain't nobody around here but us." She waved the notion away. "They'll be okay where they're at until we get to them."

Elsie pulled Libby up the steps and into the kitchen, a large, cheerful room with wall-to-wall cupboards, yellow curtains, a large black refrigerator, and several doorways leading to other sections of the house. To her left, three young women were setting the table.

"Girls," she said in a loud, but friendly manner, "this is Olivia."

"Most people call me Libby, so that's what I go by," Libby said quickly. The last thing she wanted was to be called by her legal name. It reminded her too much of Norma's constant criticism and scorn.

Elsie pointed to a petite blonde with straight, shoulder-length hair wearing a peach sundress. "This is Lindsay Bryant."

Lindsay's wide, blue eyes regarded Libby with open disdain. Instead of a polite greeting, she flipped an indifferent shrug and went back to placing a fork and napkin by each plate. The girl's unfriendliness caught Libby off guard, immediately putting her on the defensive. If everyone treated her like that, the limousine might be coming back tonight to get her!

Elsie moved on to the brunette, a pretty girl with a short bob wearing navy shorts and a matching tank top. "This is Rachel Evans."

Rachel stopped setting glasses on the table and smiled briefly. "Hi," she said so quietly it sounded like a whisper. Then she looked away and resumed her table-setting duties.

Strike two, Libby thought nervously. *Did every resident here have a chip on her shoulder?*

Lastly, Elsie pointed to a tall, lanky redhead with a lion's mane of long hair wearing a gold peasant blouse under a denim jumper. She stood at the end of the table cutting the pie into wedges.

"This is Rose of Sharon Flaherty," Elsie said, pronouncing the last word of the first name as *Sha-roan*.

"Hello," the girl said in a bold but feminine voice with a heavy Southern accent. She set down her knife, wiped her palm on a kitchen towel, and stuck out her hand. "Welcome to the farm! I'm pleased to meet you. Just call me Rose, though. I hate the Sharon part." She grimaced. "The only people who call me that are my parents."

I can totally relate to that, Libby thought.

Rose pulled out a chair and gestured for Libby to sit. "You're in luck, sugah. We're just about to have dessert. I'll get another place setting."

Elsie walked away and busied herself pouring a cup of coffee.

Not knowing what else to do, Libby sat down and tried to act as though she fit in. Lindsay and Rachel took their places at the table but continued to ignore her, whispering to each other.

Rose returned with a place setting and napkin. She set it in front of Libby and sat down, waiting for Elsie to join them. After Elsie sat down and prayed over their food, Rose began serving the pie. Libby had never eaten a homemade peach pie before but the moment she tasted the first bite of the warm, sweet dessert covered with freshly whipped cream, she couldn't eat the rest fast enough to satisfy the craving in her stomach.

"I baked this myself from scratch," Rose said and forked in a mouthful. "Hmm...it's best to eat it fresh out of the oven like this with chilled whipped cream."

Lindsay gave Rose a sideways glance, arching a golden brow in annoyance. Her own serving still sat on her plate, torn apart with her fork. She glanced at Libby and scowled, then turned her back on them both.

Libby glanced at Rose with uncertainty, but Rose simply rolled her eyes and kept eating.

After they finished, everyone quietly rose from the table, scraped their dishes, and placed them in the dishwasher.

"I'll help Libby with her bags and show her to her room," Rose offered. "Come on, Libby. It's *Lindsay's* week to clean up the kitchen." She gave Lindsay a happy look and headed for the door. Once outside, she said to Libby, "Are you able to lift a bag by yourself? The bedrooms are on the second floor."

"Sure," Libby said with a chuckle. "I may be having a baby, but I'm certainly not one myself."

They easily hauled both of her suitcases upstairs. Rose halted at the top of the stairs and pointed to the right. "Your room is in the corner over there."

The open hallway made a U-shape around the stairs. There were four bedrooms on the second floor and two bathrooms. Rose, the only lucky one in the bunch, had a small balcony in the front of the house connected to her room. Libby glanced through Rose's bedroom and saw an open screen door on the opposite side of the square room. Outside, the balcony looked large enough to hold two folding chairs.

As they hauled Libby's bags into her room, she took in her new space for the next five months. The room had a full-sized bed with one small nightstand, a dresser, two windows covered with pink curtains, and a small closet. The freshly painted eggshell walls and wide, dark-stained woodwork reminded her of Medley's house.

With a tired sigh, Rose collapsed across the handmade pink and white quilt on Libby's bed and rolled onto her back, her thick coppery hair fanning out on the bed like a large halo. "It's a plain room, but you can fix it up." She pointed to the round, pink rug on the floor with a grin. "At least *you* have a large rug in front of your bed."

Libby leaned against the dark oak dresser with an attached mirror. "At least *you* have a balcony."

They stared at each other for a moment then burst out laughing.

"I'm three months along," Rose offered in a friendly tone. "How about you?"

"I'm four and a half months along."

Rose stared at her in disbelief. "My goodness, you don't look like it! I can barely see your baby bump."

Libby laughed. "Yeah, but I'm not as skinny as I used to be. My waistline was the first thing to go."

"It feels like we're at Girl Scout camp or something," Rose said, staring at the ceiling, "except that we don't have to sleep in bunk beds and put our shoes on to go to the bathroom." She gestured with her hand at the smallness of the room. "Not to brag or anything, but my walk-in

108

closet at home is bigger than this."

Libby giggled. "Mine, too, and it's full of clothes I can't wear."

Rose stared at her for a moment as if lost in thought. Then a small tear escaped from the corner of her eye and dripped past her temple. "It's so depressing, isn't it? No cute clothes or spiked heels for the next six months. I'll probably get so fat Elsie will have to make me a muumuu from flour sacks."

She rolled over onto her stomach, resting her chin on the heels of her hands. "Oh, why, oh, why did I do it?"

Libby approached the bed. "Because you were in love?"

Rose sat up and placed her hand across her abdomen. "Can't do that anymore; lay on my stomach. It makes me queasy." She looked up. "Yes, I was in love, sinfully in love, as my daddy says. Unfortunately for me, I still am. How about you?"

Libby sat down on the bed and let out a deep sigh. "Yeah, me, too," she replied as a hollow feeling welled inside her. "I tried to call my fiancé before I left but I couldn't get ahold of him. He doesn't even know I'm here. He thinks we're going to get married as soon as I tell my dad about the baby."

"What happened?" Rose shoved a pillow behind her and scooted her back against the sleigh-style headboard. "Your daddy must have gone ballistic about having a baby when you told him, or you wouldn't be here."

Libby fluffed up a pillow and scooted toward the headboard. "I actually didn't get the chance to tell him," she said as she sat back and pulled her knees to her chest. "My grandma figured it out and *ratted* on me. He came home from Washington, D.C. to confront me about it and said I couldn't keep the baby because I was only sixteen. I didn't know it, but by that time, he'd already arranged for me to live here. On the way to Barna, the chauffer told me that my reservation for the limo had been put on their schedule a week ago."

"Wow, he moved fast." She looked Libby straight in the eyes. "Miss Elsie has a sterling reputation for her discretion in boarding girls like us. She may talk like a country lady, but she's a smart businesswoman who knows how to handle temperamental girls and at the same time, keep our information private. Even so, I'd like to know, if you don't mind saying so, what your daddy does for a living. I mean, flying home from D.C. just to talk to you makes him sound like a pretty important man."

Libby didn't hesitate. "He's a United States Senator and chair of the Senate Intelligence Committee. He spends most of his time in Washington." She let out a deep sigh. "I hardly know him."

Rose's eyes widened in surprise as she studied Libby. "And your mom? What does she do?"

Libby stretched out her legs and stared at her red-painted toenails. "She died years ago. I've spent most of my life in boarding schools and private summer camps." She stared at Rose. "Your turn. Why were you banished to Barna, Minnesota, the boondocks of America? Who's *your* daddy?"

Rose pointed to a tiny cross pendant on a gold chain around her neck. "Ever heard of Jimmy Flaherty, the television evangelist?" At Libby's nod, she said, "That's my daddy."

Libby thoughtfully considered Rose's answer. "Is he the one who does the miracle healing and deliverance services on TV?"

Rose made a face. "Yep, he's the one."

"Yikes," Libby declared with surprise, "and I thought *I* lived in a fishbowl. What about the other girls—Lindsay and Rachel?"

Rose climbed off the bed and tiptoed to the doorway. Satisfied that they were the only people upstairs, she closed the door and climbed onto the bed again. "I overheard Miss Elsie talking to Rachel about her

110

parents," she whispered as she leaned close. "They have a talk show on a Christian network and now they've also started a church. They don't want anyone to know she's having a baby out of wedlock because it would destroy their reputation, so they sent her here to keep it out of the news. She told Miss Elsie they're really upset with her."

Libby thought about that for a moment. "Do you think that's why she doesn't talk much?"

Rose nodded. "Probably." She raised one brow. "Rachel and I are both seventeen. And then there's *Lindsay*. Did you know she's nineteen? Her parents didn't force her to come here. They don't even know about the baby. She's here on her own. Her parents think she's spending time in Toronto with a friend."

Libby found that surprising. "Really? But what is she going to do about going home for holidays and family get-togethers?"

Rose ran her fingers through her long hair and stopped at a tangled knot. "Her parents are entertainers, and they travel all of the time," she said, pulling the knot apart. "They've just signed a contract with a cruise line and for the next twelve months, they'll be flying around the world, performing on all of the cruise line's ships."

"If Lindsay booked this place on her own," Libby said in puzzlement, "why does she act like she doesn't want to be here?"

Rose laughed. "Because she *doesn't* want to be here, dahlin'! I don't, either. Do you?"

"I just want to be with Cash," Libby said wistfully and grabbed her purse. She unzipped it and rummaged inside it for her date book. When she found the book, she pulled out a color photograph of him and showed it to Rose.

"Wow, what a hunk," Rose said as she studied the picture. "He looks like my favorite kind of bad boy with all that black hair. His five o'clock shadow is sooo sexy! No wonder you're having a hard time letting him go. Do you think he'll stay faithful until you come back home?"

"Of course he will," Libby said curtly. "He told me he can't imagine his life without me. My dad says I can't see him anymore, but once I turn eighteen, we're going to get married." She pulled the black velvet ring box from the pocket of her light blue twill shorts. "Cash gave this to me the day before my dad came home. He said that someday he plans to give me a bigger one." She opened the box and held it out for Rose's inspection. Then she slipped it on her finger. "I'll love him 'til the day I die."

"Well," Rose said as she returned the photo, "I wish you the best of luck. At least you have some privacy. I'll never have a life of my own unless I move away from New Orleans."

Libby snapped the empty box shut and dropped it into her purse. "Where do you plan to go?"

"As far away as I can get from Jimmy Flaherty Ministries! Believe me, you have no idea what it's like to be a PK."

Libby frowned. "A *what*?"

"A preacher's kid!" Rose slid to the edge of the bed, her bare feet dropping to the floor with a soft thud. "Everything you say, do, and wear is subject to scrutiny and provides juicy fodder for gossip. Everyone else gets away with falling into temptation, but when you're a preacher's kid, there is no forgiveness for being human. I mean, God forgives you, but *people* don't. You're expected to be absolutely perfect all the time or it reflects badly on the preacher." She sighed. "I just want to be me." She stared down at her stomach. "In six months, I'll be skinny again and eighteen—and I am moving on!"

Libby set her purse on the floor and grabbed a pillow, hugging it like a stuffed bear. "Does it bother you to know that one day you're going to give birth to a sweet little baby and then you're going to lose that child?"

112

Rose looked down for a moment. When she looked up again, her deep-set jade eyes reflected guilt and sadness. "Of course, it does. What kind of person would I be if I didn't care about my own child? But there's no way I can keep my baby because if I do, it'll bring shame and embarrassment to my parents. I hate being caught in the middle, but I have no power to change things. My only hope is that someday God will bring us together again."

Suddenly they heard Elsie's voice echoing up the stairs. "Rose, are you and Libby up there?"

Rose stood and opened the door. "Yes, ma'am," she said and grabbed one of Libby's suitcases. "We're unpacking her things." She unzipped the bag and threw open the top flap.

"You can do that later," Elsie said in an authoritative tone. "It's time to help Rachel prepare dinner."

"Coming!" Rose turned to Libby. "Rachel and I are assigned to cook this week. Guess you'll have to unpack by yourself. See you at six."

*   *   *

A few days later, Libby had her first doctor appointment. Elsie scheduled all the girls for morning appointments the same day and piled everyone into her van, heading north for a fifteen-minute ride to the town where the doctor and hospital were located. Libby's physical examination, blood work, and urine samples were routine fare, but without Cash by her side, she felt lonely and out of place.

She'd called him every night since she'd come to live with Elsie, but the phone always defaulted to a message machine. The last time she called, someone did answer, but it turned out to be his mother, Maggie, who coldly told her—

"Cash is not home and don't call here ever again...*goodbye*."

Days turned into weeks as life at the farm plodded on. Libby rotated tasks every week with the other girls, cooking with a partner—usually Rose, doing dishes, and cleaning. Everyone had to weed the garden, take turns cutting the grass with the riding mower, and tend to the animals, but Libby didn't mind outdoor work like the other girls did. It gave her a chance to get fresh air and do things she'd never done before, like collecting eggs, picking strawberries, or pulling up a handful of fresh radishes for dinner.

Still, it did nothing to ease the loneliness that lurked in every corner of her heart.

"What are you going to do with your life after you've done your time here?" Rose asked her one night as they relaxed in lawn chairs on her tiny balcony, nibbling on chocolate chip cookies from a batch they'd made that afternoon.

Libby reached into the large green Tupperware bowl and selected another one. "I'm going to finish my last two years of school then marry Cash." Her answer sounded muffled as she bit into the cookie, savoring the taste of rich chocolate and buttery brown sugar in her mouth.

"Have you talked to him lately?" Rose asked boldly.

"No." Libby glanced at her friend, wondering why she wanted to know. "Not since the last time we met at Sandhill Nature Center. It's a park with tall cottonwood trees and walking paths around a small lake. We used to meet there after school because the woods gave us privacy and it's close to my house."

"Why did you stop calling his house every night?"

Libby brushed a crumb from her lap, becoming uncomfortable with the direction Rose obviously meant to steer the subject. "I gave up." She didn't mention her run-in with Maggie. It was too embarrassing.

Rose's expression went into a serious mode. "If that boy hasn't called you back by now, I do believe he's not going to."

In her heart, Libby already suspected this but hearing the truth out loud made her mad. "Yes, he will!"

Rose gave her a stern look. "No, he won't, and we both know it. It's time you grew up, Miss Libby, and accepted the truth. You don't want to give up on him, but sugah, in your heart you know he's already given up on you."

Losing her appetite, Libby threw the rest of her cookie over the balcony into the darkness beyond. "You're wrong about Cash. He told me he'd always love me. He wouldn't change his mind about me."

Sadly, even as the words came out, she heard the doubt overshadowing her voice, making her more upset.

Rose turned in her chair to face Libby. "Please, listen to what I'm saying." A golden shaft of light from her room reflected upon her pale, freckled face, her jade eyes showing genuine concern. "I'm not trying to hurt your feelings, but you're clinging to something that ended before you came here, and you can't do anything about it except let it go so it doesn't have the power to hurt you anymore. That boy has moved on, and you need to move on, too."

"But, Rose," Libby argued in desperation, "he's all I have."

"Then it's time you took control of your life, girl, and like my daddy says, get a new vision for your future," Rose lectured. "You can't keep living in the past. It's over. You need to leave him behind and move on or it'll drive you crazy."

Not until I've talked to Cash, Libby thought defiantly. *I need to hear it from him.*

But it had been a month since the last time she'd spoken to him. Had he forgotten her by now? Or had he simply given up on her? She didn't know the answer and that was why she couldn't give up on him. *Ever.*

Chapter Twelve

Cash sat in his car across the street from Libby's house, anxious to catch a glimpse of her. He'd agreed not to approach her, but no one ever said he couldn't watch her from afar. Or talk to her if *she* approached him. He desperately needed to know how she was faring. Was the baby healthy? Was she feeling okay? Most of all, he needed to hear—from her—if she *really* didn't want to see him any longer.

Libby's bedroom on the second floor faced the street. The sheer curtains in her window were drawn but no light shone through them. For that matter, the entire house looked deserted. Even so, if he could gather solid proof that she was home, he'd find a way to reach out to her. All he wanted was to see her one more time and hear from *her* lips that she didn't want anything to do with him any longer. After all they'd been through together, he *needed* to know why. He needed closure. It would hurt, but he'd deal with it. Where had she gone?

He sat watching the house for another fifteen minutes, wondering if she stood behind the sheer curtains covering her window, watching him. If so, she made no effort to let him know. Disappointed, he started the car and drove home, his morale sinking lower than ever. His heart ached over their breakup, especially the way it came about.

"I don't believe she doesn't want to see me anymore," he

mumbled angrily to himself. "I know her better than anyone does! She loves me. And I love her." He exhaled a long, tired sigh. "And that's why I can't let this go. Not yet anyway. If she tells me to my face that we're done, I'll never bother her again. Ever. Until then, I'm not giving up."

At home, Barney met him at the car, wagging his tail and whining for attention. Cash gave the dog some needed ear-rubbing and made his way to the kitchen door in the back of the house.

Maggie stood at the counter, talking on the telephone when he entered. Engrossed in a serious conversation, she didn't notice him at first.

"Well, I hated to be so abrupt, but I had to put my foot down and end it or risk him being here when—" She glanced up. Startled by his presence, she pushed herself away from the edge of the counter and cleared her throat. "Gosh, look at the time. I need to get dinner on the table, so I'll let you go. Thanks for calling. All right, bye."

"Who were you talking to," Cash asked curiously.

"No one important," Maggie said as she quickly hung up the phone and walked to the refrigerator. "We're having potato salad and grilled burgers for dinner. I've got a couple of brats cooking on the grill for you and Dad, too." She pulled out a plate of freshly made hamburger patties. "Dad is in the living room watching the news. Tell him dinner will be ready in fifteen minutes." She shut the refrigerator door and paused, a guilty expression crossing her face. "What are you staring at? Go. Take your shower so you don't hold up dinner. These burgers won't take long."

Surprised at her abruptness, Cash left the kitchen and headed upstairs, relaying Maggie's message to Ray on the way. Up in his room, he pulled his shirt off and shoved it into the clothes chute, mulling over her odd response to his question. He could always tell when she wasn't being truthful—which didn't happen often—but he had no doubt he'd just caught her in a lie. The hard stare, the curt response, and the busyness to distance herself from the situation gave her away.

Who had she been talking to on the phone? Who had caused her to put her foot down and respond with abruptness? Why did she feel the need to cover it up? A wave of uneasiness stirred in his soul. His family didn't withhold secrets from each other and that was why both of his parents were upset when they found out about Libby. That also was why Maggie's uncharacteristic behavior looked suspicious. What was she holding back?

It made him more determined than ever to find out what was *really* going on with Libby.

*　*　*

Cash drove over to Libby's house on Saturday morning and parked across the street, determined to sit there all day if need be, to find out what he could about Libby. Every idea he'd tried so far had turned up nothing. Libby's friends didn't have a clue as to where she'd gone. He'd tried to get in touch with Medley, but her mother said she had gone to an art camp for the entire summer. When he asked Mrs. Grant about Libby, the woman gave him a vague answer. Something on the order of, "Gosh, I have no idea what my niece is up to these days…"

The garbage got picked up this morning, so Delores Lopez, the housekeeper, had to be there to roll the bin into the garage. He planned to approach her and ask her about Libby. He'd stocked the car with a couple of sports magazines, a small cooler filled with cola, and a jumbo bag of chips to tide him over as he waited. When he arrived, he found the black bin, tall and rectangular, sitting at the curb as usual, waiting for service.

Thankfully, the senator and his paid goons were in Washington. Cash saw Frank Cunningham on the news last night, speaking at the capitol about a budget bill.

At ten-fifteen, the garbage truck pulled up and emptied the bin.

At ten-thirty, Delores came out of the house and walked down the driveway to retrieve it. The petite woman had short, dark hair and wore a plain green dress. Apprehensive, but hopeful that she would be receptive to him, Cash jumped out of his car and slowly walked toward her.

"Excuse me," he said politely as he approached her. "I've been by a few times, and no one seems to be home. I'm worried about Libby. Where has she gone?"

She paused, eyeing him suspiciously. "Why do you want to know?"

"I haven't seen her for almost a month, and I need to know that she's okay," he blurted. "I-I'm a friend."

Delores gripped her fingers around the wide handle of the bin and stared at him with a disapproving frown. "I know who you *are*. You're not allowed to see her anymore. You shouldn't be here."

Cash shoved his hands into his pockets and stepped closer, keeping his voice down. "Please, I'm not looking to cause any trouble. I just want to know how she's getting along and…and if the baby is okay. I never got to say goodbye to her, and I miss her. I *love* her."

"I'm sorry, she's not here," Delores replied, her voice softening. "I don't know where she is or when she'll be back. All I can tell you is that she's been gone for nearly a month. The day the senator came home and confronted her about you, I was told to pack her bags. They had quite a showdown. The next morning, a limo showed up at the house to take her somewhere. I haven't seen or talked to her since." Delores glanced toward the house and sighed as if to see the instant replay in her mind. "They're all gone." She turned back to him. "The senator went back to Washington D.C. the next morning. Mrs. Cunningham flew out there a few days ago. I haven't heard from anyone since they left."

Cash's heart fell to his feet. "Did Libby say anything to you about me?"

"No," she replied and shook her head. "I didn't get a chance to speak with her after the screaming match she had with her father."

Cash stared at the ground, upset and angry that Libby had to face her father by herself. "Something is wrong. I just know it. She wouldn't have left without getting a message to me. I'm more worried about her now than ever."

"Don't give up on her. Wherever Miss Libby is staying right now," Delores said as she placed her hand reassuringly on his arm, "I'm sure she's doing fine. She's a resilient young lady."

"I hope so." Cash slowly turned and walked away, more depressed than ever. Libby gone without a trace? For a moment, he wondered if Delores was simply repeating what Norma Cunningham had instructed her to say, but the sincerity in the woman's voice convinced him that she'd told him the truth.

"You take care now, Mr. MacKenzie," Delores said as he walked away. "If she comes home, I'll tell her that you came by and asked about her."

He waved goodbye but didn't look back. He couldn't speak. He had all he could do to keep the knot in his throat from choking him.

* * *

July Fourth

Cash sat in a chaise lounge sipping a bottle of Coke, keeping to himself as the family picnic carried on around him. He couldn't quit thinking about Libby. Questions swirled in his head about her whereabouts and why she hadn't tried to contact him, but he had no answers because he had no one to turn to for help.

The pungent aroma of sizzling brats and burgers wafted from across the patio where Ray and one of Cash's uncles stood working the grill. At the same time, Maggie and a few of the women were busily setting up a large outdoor buffet with salads, chips, veggies, sliced watermelon, and desserts. Next to the garage, a half-dozen swimsuit-clad children happily danced and splashed around in a molded swimming pool. Cash kept a close eye on them, having been designated a makeshift lifeguard by his mother.

"Hey, Cash!"

He glanced up to see one of his cousins walking toward him. "What's up, Tom?"

The tall, skinny teen with tousled red hair wore cutoffs and a gray T-shirt. As he approached Cash, a wide grin spread across his face. "There's a free concert and fireworks at Boom Island tonight. Wanna go?"

Cash shrugged and glanced at the kiddie pool. He didn't really feel like it today.

"Aw, c'mon, buddy," Tom said with a coaxing thread in his voice. "I'm supposed to pick up my girlfriend, Alicia at six. Jodi wants to come too, but she doesn't have a date and she feels stupid tagging along with us. If you come along, we'll be evenly matched. Besides," he said, glancing toward the adults to make sure they weren't listening. "Chillin' with your cousins is a lot more fun than hanging out with a bunch of old married people and screaming kids."

"Hey, you!" Cash sat up and pointed toward one of the kids in the pool. "Danny! No fighting! And no pushing, got that?" He slumped back down in his chair again and looked up at Tom, trying to come up with an excuse to get out of escorting Tom's younger sister, Jodi, to the fireworks. "I don't know. I hear it's going to get cloudy around dinnertime and it might rain."

"Yeah, but not until late," Tom argued. "With any luck, we'll miss the rain completely. C'mon, it'll be fun!"

"That sounds like a great idea, Tom," Maggie said as she came up behind them. "Lunch will be ready as soon as the meat is done so you kids will have plenty of time after the picnic to pick up your friend and make it to the concert. In the meantime, Tom, why don't you help yourself to a soda? We've got lots of chilled Mountain Dew."

"Great! Thanks, Aunt Maggie. I'll get one." Tom grinned at Cash. "Okay then, we'll leave here at five-thirty to pick up Alicia. I'll tell Jodi that you're coming with us." He turned and walked toward a line of coolers stuffed with everything from juice boxes and lemonade to soda.

Startled, Cash sat up and twisted in his seat. Maggie wiped her hands on her red, white, and blue striped apron. He knew the real reason why she wanted him to go. "Keeping me busy isn't going to change the way I feel," he said as soon as Tom moved out of earshot. "I need to know what's going on with Libby and I'm not going to stop pursuing the truth until I do."

Maggie's friendly demeanor turned into a worried frown at the mention of Libby's name. "Honey, I know you're upset about the way things turned out, but you can't go anywhere near that young lady," she whispered and nervously glanced around. "This isn't the time or place to be discussing this and frankly, I don't know what else there is to say that hasn't already been said. You agreed to leave her alone and if you go back on your word, you'll face retribution from Senator Cunningham. Is that what you want?" She placed her hand on his shoulder. "Look, it's a beautiful day for celebrating and there are a lot of people here that we won't see again until next year so put it behind you for now and go to the fireworks with your cousins. Enjoy yourself!"

With that, she turned and stalked away, leaving Cash to simmer quietly with frustration. After a few minutes of mulling over her words of encouragement, he rolled out of the chaise lounge and went over to the pool with a stack of towels to round up the kids for lunch. She was right about keeping their family business private. The last thing he wanted to do was hurt Libby's reputation and embarrass his parents as well.

But ignoring the issue didn't fix his problem or make him feel any better. The only solution he knew that would set his heart at rest was to find Libby and talk to her.

Cash volunteered to drive his car to the event, but he had to stop for gas along the way. After they picked up Tom's girlfriend, they stopped at a local service station and Cash jumped out to fill up his car.

Tom and Alicia stayed in the back seat, holding hands and whispering to each other. Jodi sat in the front seat with him, but she got out of the car and went into the station to get an ice-cold fountain drink while he filled the tank.

He stood holding the nozzle and staring at the pump when something cold and wet slithered down his back. What the...? "Ah-h-h-h!"

Jodi began laughing uncontrollably. Reaching into her tall cup, she withdrew another chunk of ice and threw it at him.

"Hey!" He left the nozzle in the tank and merrily chased her around the car. "Two can play at this game!"

She quickly jerked open the car door and jumped in, slamming the door after her and setting the lock.

"I owe you one!" Cash bellowed, but at the same time, he couldn't help laughing.

Suddenly, he froze. Looking across the roof of the car he caught a glimpse of a slim, dark-haired girl getting into a white SUV. A girl that looked a lot like Medley Grant. He stared hard at her retreating form, trying to get a better look at her face, but the door shut before he could clearly make out her features. He kept staring as the car backed out of its parking space and left the station, wondering if she saw him, too. If she recognized him, wouldn't she have called to him and waved?

Shaking his head, he pulled the nozzle from his car and screwed on the gas cap. *It's probably just my imagination,* he thought with disappointment and placed the nozzle back on the gas pump.

He got back into his car and drove to the concert, knowing he'd spend the entire night watching the crowd for a glimpse of Medley and Libby.

Chapter Thirteen

As the summer progressed, Libby settled into life on the farm and adjusted to the changes taking place in her body. Morning sickness no longer plagued her. She'd gained her appetite back, including a craving for sweets. A small tummy had begun to protrude from her abdomen, and she experienced a fluttering motion whenever the baby moved inside her.

Contrary to her first impression, life at Elsie's farm proved to be anything but dull. Elsie expected her rules to be obeyed but they weren't onerous, and she liberally gave out hugs of appreciation and praise to the girls for all their hard work.

Libby spent her days outdoors in the garden tending to Elsie's beautiful flowers or reading romance books in a shady hammock. Her evenings were spent around the dining room table, playing games, or working on a large puzzle. She learned to cook, bake, and leave the kitchen as spotless as she found it. Doctor appointments were on Wednesdays, and church on Sundays. On Tuesdays, they shopped, dined out, and went to the movies in a nearby town.

Best of all, Libby loved sitting with Rose on her deck after dark enjoying the balmy summer nights. They had to wear a lot of mosquito lotion, but the inconvenience was worth it. She enjoyed their honest, often-spirited talks about everything from family to school to the boys that they loved.

"You need to thank Him, you know," Rose said late one evening in mid-August. They'd managed to squeeze two chaise lounges onto the balcony and bundled up in homemade quilts under the stars, watching long "wakes" of blue-white light streak across the inky black sky from the Perseid meteor shower.

Libby shifted in her chair to grab her water bottle. "Thank who?"

"God, of course," Rose replied curtly.

Libby responded with a sharp laugh. "What for?"

"For bringing you here." Rose reached into a crinkling bag of caramels and tossed one onto Libby's lap. "You don't think it was by accident that you ended up in this place, do you? God put someone in your papa's path to tell him about Elsie's farm. Everything God orchestrates is for your good, you know."

"I'm not so sure about that," Libby said as she unwrapped the caramel and popped it into her mouth. "Is that why the last year of my life has been such a disaster? Because God is doing it for my good?"

"Listen, pumpkin," Rose lectured, her Southern accent deepening. "*You* got yourself kicked out of one of the most prestigious Christian schools in the country for repeatedly defying their rules. *You're* the one who got yourself in trouble fooling around with a boy. It's not God's fault that you made those bad choices."

"Yeah, but—"

"I know, I know." Rose held up her hand to silence Libby's protest. "The people you trusted let you down when you needed it the most, but that's not God's fault, either. Your papa chose to pay others to raise you, and your nana makes the Wicked Witch of the West sound like a nun. They choose to think and act the way they do and one day they will answer for that, but in the meantime, you need to forgive them and get on with your life."

Libby threw her empty caramel wrapper at Rose. "Why should I?"

"For your own sake," Rose said, her voice softening. "Holding resentment in your heart is only hurting you. The people who sent you here are getting on with their lives. You should, too."

"I guess you're right about that," Libby replied sadly. "Medley and Aunt Barbara are the only people who stay in touch with me. It's as if everyone else has forgotten about me." *Especially Cash*, she thought as her heart crashed to her feet.

"I didn't want to come here," Rose confessed. "I threw a hissy fit when my daddy told me where he was sending me. I didn't want to spend six months of my life on some old farm smelling like cow manure and dirt. I knew he was banishing me to salvage his reputation and it made me resentful, but you know what? I don't feel that way anymore. I'm *glad* I'm here." Placing her arm across the back of her chair, she gazed up at the stars. "I can be myself here. Nobody is gossiping about me behind my back or criticizing the way I dress. And for the first time in my life, I have someone I can pour my heart out to. Someone who listens with an open mind and doesn't judge me."

Libby laughed. "Yes! Me, too! You're so easy to talk to and you always tell me the truth."

Rose quickly placed her hand on Libby's shoulder. "I feel the same way about you, too, honey, but I'm talking about Elsie. She's become like a mother to me."

Libby popped the caramel into her mouth and savored the sweet, buttery taste. "You're right. I've never been hugged so much in my life. At first, I thought she was just pretending to be sympathetic but now that I know her better, I *know* she cares."

"Elsie is like my second mother," Rose said as she settled back in her chair and pulled her quilt to her chin.

Libby nodded as she spoke, her voice muffled from a mouthful of thick, creamy caramel. "Well, since I never had one growing up, she's the *only* mother I've ever known."

Rose cast her a sideways glance. "Have you talked to Elsie about Cash? She knows you're writing letters to him. Everybody does."

Libby let out a long sigh and stretched out under her quilt. After Cash's mother ordered her to never call him again, she realized the only alternative she had to let him know what happened to her was to write to him. Surely, he was getting her letters. Why hadn't he contacted her? She'd sent him a half-dozen so far.

"Not yet," she replied. "I know Elsie doesn't approve of it. She thinks I should accept the MacKenzies' decision to cut me off from their son and move on, but Elsie doesn't understand how much it hurts not to have closure. Nobody does..."

She tipped her head back and stared up at the star-studded sky. "I don't want to give up my baby, Rose. I know Cash wants the baby too, and he would back me up if he knew what I'm going through. Don't you ever wonder if you're doing the right thing?"

"I don't have to wonder about it, I *know* I'm doing the right thing," Rose said with finality. "It may not be what I want, but it's the right decision for my family and the baby. No matter where she is placed, I'm darn sure she's going to grow up with a happier, more carefree childhood than I did." Rose leaned toward Libby and grabbed her hand. "I know it hurts. It hurts me, too. We'll get through this together."

Libby gripped Rose's fingers and swallowed hard, too choked up to answer.

Chapter Fourteen

Early September

Anxiously waiting for the arrival of her guests, Libby straightened the silky gold tablecloth on the dining room table as Lindsay placed a large vase of fresh-cut flowers in the center. The girls had been working for two days, mowing and trimming the lawn, preparing food, and cleaning the farmhouse in anticipation of their "Family Day" event. She'd dressed casually today in white cotton leggings and a light blue top with white trim. Rose had woven a blue ribbon along with her long blonde hair into a loose French braid and adorned it with tiny rhinestone clips.

Medley and Aunt Barbara had accepted her invitation and were due to arrive any minute now. However, Rachel's parents, Lynne and Bill Evans, Christian talk show hosts who'd recently also started a church, were the first guests to arrive. They pulled up in a black rented Cadillac wearing casual clothes and sunglasses. Rachel's mother wore a floppy-brimmed hat covering her dark hair. Her father had on a black bill cap pulled down so low it nearly covered his eyes.

After greeting their daughter and introducing themselves to Elsie, they stood in the kitchen, silently staring around as though they found the situation extremely awkward. Elsie appeared to take their discomfort in stride and welcomed them as though she didn't notice anything was amiss. After introductions, she offered them a cool beverage and proceeded to chat with them as though they were old friends.

Rose's grandmother, Millicent Flaherty, arrived next, wearing a dark, shawl-collared suit with a frilly white blouse and a large, brimmed hat with an ostrich feather plume. She entered the kitchen slowly, leaning heavily on her cane. The stooped, gray-haired lady had a regal, commanding air about her suggesting that she was used to being in control of every situation. A middle-aged companion who spoke in deep tones, and only with her, followed behind her. The nondescript woman took great care to see that Millicent had a comfortable chair to sit in and quickly attended to her every need. Both wore dour expressions and spoke with a strong Southern accent. Both were polite, but their rigidness discouraged even the briefest of conversation.

Rose fluttered about, chattering and giggly, trying to soften the austerity of her grandmother's presence. Millicent snapped at her, telling her to sit down and mind her manners.

Another car pulled into the driveway. Libby ran to the screen door to see if Medley had arrived, but it wasn't the Grant family vehicle. A small red sports car pulled into a shady space under a large maple tree and a tall, slender blonde emerged; a young woman who looked identical to Lindsay, only a few years older. She wore designer clothes, carried a Louis Vuitton handbag, and glanced around the farmhouse property with an air of entitlement. Rushing past her, Lindsay flew out the kitchen door, letting it shut with a bang as she ran to greet her sister, Brianna.

Libby turned away in disappointment. Where were they? Barbara had a thing about promptness. Why was she late?

"Don't worry, honey," Elsie whispered in her ear as she slid her arm around Libby's shoulders. "They called me as soon as they got the invitation and confirmed they were coming. Have patience, they'll be here." Elsie gave her a quick hug and then handed her a green depression glass snack plate filled with taco dip and chips. "Here, put these on the table next to the veggie plate.

Fifteen minutes later, Aunt Barbara's SUV pulled off the county road onto the long sandy driveway. Once they pulled into the space next to Brianna's car, Libby ran to meet them, hugging them both and telling them how much she missed them.

"I'm so sorry we're late," Medley said with true regret in her voice. "We used the GPS to find this place, but we still got mixed up on the freeway and took the wrong exit."

"That's okay. At least you made it!" Libby turned to her aunt. "Is Dad coming?"

"Your father sends his regrets," Barbara said dryly, sounding irritated as she grabbed her purse from the back seat of the car. "He says wanted to come, but he had several high-level cabinet meetings this week. And so, duty *calls*."

"And duty comes first, as usual," Libby replied quickly. Even though she found it disappointing, she couldn't help smiling. "You're here and I'm so glad to see you!" She led them into the house to meet Elsie and introduce them to her companions and their guests. Barbara got along famously with Elsie, laughing and cracking jokes about getting lost even with GPS. Together they lightened the mood and encouraged others to engage in the conversation.

The girls served lunch at one o'clock, a light meal of sandwiches and salads followed by a round of heavenly desserts. Each girl made her favorite item, filling the table with brownies, Rice Krispie bars, chocolate chip cookies, and homemade frosted cupcakes.

Libby had a sweet craving for Elsie's chocolate syrup homemade brownies, but she decided on Elsie's no-bake Rice Krispie bars. The soft, chewy treat made with marshmallow crème had a layer of thick, creamy caramel in the center. While cutting the pieces in the morning, she and Rose crammed a couple of gooey chunks into their mouths and giggled so much that Elsie had to intervene, gently but firmly telling them to stop horsing around and get to work.

After lunch, Libby and Medley took a walk around the property and eventually ended up at the large pond down the hill from the house. The girls had cleared a walking path on the riding mower all around it so they could watch the Mallards and occasionally a few swans. They began to walk around the pond.

"Have you talked to Cash?" Libby asked anxiously.

Medley's eyes widened as though the question alarmed her. She swallowed hard and gave Libby a guilty stare. "No. Have you?"

"I tried calling him, but his mother wouldn't let me speak to him. She claimed he wasn't home." Libby bit her lip in frustration. "The last time, she told me never to call there again. I've written him letters, but he hasn't responded."

Two large turtles sunning themselves slipped off a floating log into the water, making a noticeable splash. They disappeared into a patch of cattails. Libby let out a loud sigh as she and Medley walked past the empty log bobbing on the water. "I don't believe he doesn't want to talk to me," she complained. "The last time we were together everything was great between us."

Holding out her hand, she examined the promise ring he'd given her and then held it up for Medley's inspection. "He gave me this and told me he'd always love me. Medley, I can't give up on him now. Knowing that one day we'll meet again is the only thing that keeps me going."

Medley slowed down her pace and stared at the ground as she walked. "I need to tell you something. I—I have bad news."

Medley's remorse Libby stopped in her tracks. "What? What news?" Her heart began to race. "What happened?"

"Well...it's..." Medley said, her eyes rife with sadness. "I wish I wouldn't have seen it, but because I did, I can't keep it to myself. You have the right to know."

"What happened?" Libby repeated on the verge of tears. "What did you see?"

"I finished the first session of art camp and came home for the weekend to celebrate the Fourth of July with Mom and Dad," Medley began. "On the way to the fireworks, Dad stopped at a gas station for Mom and me to get a couple bottles of water and…" She looked away. "I saw Cash."

Libby nearly fainted. "You did? Oh, my gosh, but you said you haven't talked to him!"

Medley began walking again—fast this time. "No, I didn't. I ducked into the car before he saw me. He…he was with another girl."

Libby whirled around and grabbed Medley by the arm, panicking. Her heart began to slam in her chest. "What girl? Who was she?"

"I don't know," Medley replied. "She must not have been from our school because I didn't recognize her. I *did* recognize his car right away. She and Cash were together because I saw another couple sitting in the back. I only saw them for a few seconds as we drove away, but she and Cash were standing next to the car joking around and laughing. It was obvious they were together."

Medley's news shocked Libby so badly that she couldn't speak at first.

"It hurts me to break your heart like this, Libby," Medley said in a rush. "It really does, but you have the right to know the truth about him. He's not coming to the phone or answering your letters because he's with someone else now."

Cash with someone else? How could he? After the promises he'd made to her, after everything they'd been through together—did it mean nothing to him? Libby blinked hard, holding back the tears that threatened to fall and make her more miserable than she already was. A hard lump formed in her throat.

"All of those letters I wrote to him," she said, struggling to get the words out. "Pouring my heart out to him. He probably just threw them away. I wonder if he even opened them." She turned away and stared at a bumblebee climbing all over a tall goldenrod. "What a fool I've been," she managed to whisper. "He told me he'd love me always. I believed him. I *trusted* him." She shook her head. "I wish I'd never met him."

With tears in her eyes, Medley slipped her arms around Libby and held her close. "I wish I'd never introduced him to you."

"It's not your fault," Libby replied with a sniffle. "Neither one of us knew it would come to this."

They finished their walk around the pond and made their way back to the house. Libby and Medley spent the afternoon playing croquet with Rose, Rachel, Lindsay, and Brianna. The girls formed three teams and competed for a small trophy filled with fancy chocolates. Libby and Medley came in third place. Neither had the heart for it now.

The party ended at four o'clock in the afternoon. Libby walked Barbara and Medley to their car, sad to see them go. She had no idea when she would see them again.

"Listen," Barbara said, pausing against the open car door. "I've had a couple of private discussions with your father about your coming to live with us. He hasn't agreed to it yet, but he's not saying that the subject is closed either, so I think his conscience is bothering him. Don't worry, Libby, I'll keep talking to him until I change his mind."

Leave Elsie and the girls? Suddenly the idea alarmed her. They were her friends, her extended family now, her rock of support. She couldn't imagine going through labor and delivery without them. She needed them!

"I'm grateful for all that you're doing on my behalf, Auntie Barbara, but I don't want to leave this place," Libby said softly. "I'm happy here. This is where I belong—for now."

Barbara stared at her, taken aback. "All right," she replied sounding baffled and somewhat disappointed. "If that's what you want then I'll let the matter rest but if you change your mind, don't hesitate to call me. I love you, honey, and I'll support you in any way I can."

"I love you, too," Libby said in a thick voice and threw her arms around her aunt. "Thing is, I've grown close to Elsie and the girls, they're like family to me and I don't want to leave them. We need to finish this chapter of our lives together."

Libby stood in the center of the driveway and watched their car drive away until it turned onto the highway and disappeared. The other guests were leaving as well and while everyone else was preoccupied with their goodbyes, Libby slipped away and walked back down to the pond. She wanted to be alone. She had a lot to think about. Until today, she'd always believed that she and Cash would one day be reunited. Now that he'd found someone else, she didn't know what to do.

Standing on the path, she stared across the pond for a while, staring at a stand of golden aspens as tears welled up inside her. "How could you do this to me, Cash?" She began to sob aloud, letting her hurt and anger spill over. "You said you'd always love me. You said we'd always be together. What happened? How could you have forgotten me so soon?" She pulled his ring from her finger and stared at it in her palm. "This didn't mean anything to you, did it? You're a liar and a fraud, Cash MacKenzie." In a burst of anger, she pulled back her arm and threw the ring as far as she could across the pond. It landed in the water with a loud plunk. "I hate you! I wish I'd never met you!"

Covering her face with her hands she cried her heart out.

"He was never coming to save you," someone behind her declared.

135

Shocked that someone overheard her, Libby gasped and whirled toward the voice. Lindsay stood a few feet away in a yellow empire-waisted sundress next to a tall clump of wild purple asters with her arms folded, staring at Libby with a solemn expression. "It's up to *you* to save yourself. You have to be strong, Libby. It's your life. Your future and your happiness. Don't give someone else that kind of power over you."

Libby stared at her, stunned into silence. Is that what she had been doing? Giving Cash the power to make or break her happiness? "Without him, I—I feel so alone," she replied hearing the defeat in her voice as emotional exhaustion overtook her.

"But you're not alone," Lindsay said boldly as she walked toward Libby. "Elsie, Rose, Rachel, me and you—we're all in this together." She held out her hand. "You're going to be fine, okay? Come on. Let's go back to the house and talk about it. We'll have some of Elsie's strawberry-rhubarb cake with whipped cream. We're going to get through this together."

Surprised by the deep sincerity in Lindsay's words, Libby took her hand and began to walk with her. Until now, she and Lindsay had rarely discussed much beyond household chores, what to make for dinner, and their Tuesday outings, but she welcomed the older girl's concern. Being an only child, Libby didn't have anyone with which to have a "big sister" talk except Medley. However, the physical distance between them now made that almost impossible.

"I've been so obsessed with reconnecting with him again that I guess I haven't thought about much else. I have nothing to look forward to now. My future feels like a blank slate."

"So, fill it in," Lindsay said seriously. "Start making plans for what you're going to do once you leave here. Where are you going to go to school? What about college?" She smiled. "The real question is…what are you going to wear?"

Libby chuckled, letting the subject of new clothes distract her from the distress of her soul-crushing news. Eating cake wouldn't solve her problems, either, but it would satisfy her sweet tooth for now and take her mind off Cash's betrayal for at least a little while. She let go of Lindsay's hand. "Speedwalk you to the house."

Lindsay laughed. "Are you kidding? It'll mess up my hair."

"Okay, I'll wait for you by the garage." Libby sped up and began swinging her arms to move faster. She didn't care about getting exercise, she just wanted to get away from the place where she'd chucked Cash's ring to avoid thinking about it ever again.

*   *   *

Later that night, Libby lay in her bed in the darkness of her room, staring at the ceiling as her mind churned with anxious thoughts. Why did most days go by peacefully, but others could become so awful that a person would never be the same again? Bad days were always unexpected—like today. She'd looked forward to their party for several weeks but by the afternoon it had become a disaster.

"Why is my life such a mess, God?" she whispered. "What did I ever do to bring so much trouble upon myself? Okay, getting pregnant was my fault, but what did I do to make Cash abandon me? I'm truly sorry for all the problems I've caused everyone involved, especially my dad. I never meant to hurt him like I did.

"But, God, what about me? Why did my mom have to die so young and leave me all alone? And Grandma Norma—why does she hate me so much?"

She went still for a little while, waiting for an answer but when none came she began to mull over what Lindsay said about making future plans. Presently, Elsie was homeschooling her, but what would she do once the baby came?

"I'm going to make sure that wherever I go to school, it'll be as far away from here as possible," she whispered hoping that God was still listening. "I'm going to start over with new friends and a new life. Leave Minnesota and never look back. I've switched schools mid-year before. I can do it again."

She thought about leaving Cash behind as well. It hurt to accept the fact that she'd never see him again. The loving expression she'd seen so many times on his face flashed vividly through her mind. The last time they were together, his eyes had beheld hers with a passionate intensity that made her believe everything would be okay. She had no idea why he'd turned his back on her and she probably never would. His betrayal hurt so much! But even so, learning that he'd broken all his promises to her, that it was over between them forever gave her the freedom to stop worrying about him and get on with her life.

A sudden calm came over her, as though a huge weight had lifted off her. For the first time in a long time, she could go to sleep without worrying about her relationship with Cash.

She could look forward instead of backward.

Chapter Fifteen

October 19th

"O-o-o-o-h, my back hurts," Libby complained as she struggled to sit on the edge of the bed in her cotton nightgown. Besides the back pain, her bulbous stomach made it even more difficult to move around. She needed to muster enough energy to stand up, but her feet were so swollen it hurt to put her weight on them.

Rose stood over her, placing a hand on her shoulder to steady her. "I don't doubt it, Libby. Your due date was yesterday. You must be in labor." Due in a few weeks herself, Rose straightened with a grimace, placing her hands on her lower back to brace herself. "I'd better tell Elsie."

The backache began early in the morning, beginning with small twinges that increased in intensity and frequency as she lay in her bed, wondering if this was the real thing.

Elsie appeared quickly and took charge. "Can you lift your feet off the floor, Libby? I'll put your slippers on." She glanced back at Rose standing in the doorway. "Grab her overnight case, dear, and put it in the car." Turning back to Libby, Elsie began to tug her slippers on. "My goodness, it never rains but it pours. Now I've got two of you who need to go to the hospital."

Libby and Rose gasped at the same time. "Who else?" Libby

139

blurted before Rose could get the words out.

Elsie gently eased one slipper over her puffy foot. "Rachel isn't feeling well. She's downstairs lying on the sofa with cramps and because she's not due for another six weeks I'm concerned." Elsie stood and took Libby by the arm, helping her stand. "I've already got the car parked at the door. Rose, get Rachel's bag too on your way out. Lindsay is assisting her to the car."

Libby glanced out the window at the sunny fall day. The century-old oaks in Elsie's yard were past their peak of fall color but there remained a few with deep burgundy hues. A perfect day to have a baby. *Wow*, she thought excitedly. *It's really going to happen—today.* Suddenly, a dark cloud dampened her happy thoughts. As soon as she became a mother her child would be taken away.

Elsie held out her hands. "Can you stand up? All right, there you go." She helped Libby slip on her robe and tie the sash. "Now let's get you downstairs and we'll be on our way. The sooner we get to the hospital, the sooner you'll be able to see the doctor."

Libby pushed her emotions about the baby aside for now. If she thought about the situation too much, she'd start crying and she needed to be strong, both for herself and for the other girls—especially Rachel.

Once Elsie had everyone packed into the SUV she drove to the hospital, an old, one-story brick building in the next town, eleven miles away. As soon as the girls arrived, Elsie took charge like a devoted mother, communicating with the hospital staff to get the girls admitted and making sure they were comfortable before the doctor arrived. The birthing ward had only one room that was divided into two sections, so Libby and Rachel were together.

The nurse on duty determined right away that Rachel was in premature labor, and she came into the room often to check on her. Lindsay sat next to Rachel's bed, holding her hand and speaking encouraging words to her as the contractions grew stronger and closer together.

When the doctor arrived, the nurse ushered everyone out of the room. The women went to a small cafe across the street to get a soda and a snack, leaving Libby and Rachel alone as they waited for the doctor to appear.

"I'm afraid," Rachel whispered to Libby, her eyes filled with tears. "I don't want my baby to be born too soon."

"I'll pray for you," Libby said before she realized what she was promising. Would God listen to her? Would God answer her request?

Rachel reached across the narrow space between them, extending her hand. "Thank you. It means a lot to me."

Surprised by Rachel's sudden show of closeness, Libby leaned toward her and took her hand, squeezing it. Rachel had always been somewhat reserved, rarely showing emotion. But then, she was truly worried about her baby's early delivery. Libby was worried for her, too.

The doctor and a nurse entered the room, pulled the curtain between the beds, and proceeded to examine both girls one at a time. They spoke to each other in clipped tones but said little to either girl. When they left, Libby sighed. "I'm looking forward to having my baby, but when this is over, I'll be glad to go home." Home, to her, meant her own soft bed and cheerful bedroom with yellow curtains at Elsie's farmhouse. She'd begun to think of Elsie as family and her room as her own. A place where she felt safe, cared for with love, and part of a real family. For the first time in her life, she felt as if she belonged. What would she do when her time came to leave?

I just want to see my baby, she thought to herself, pushing all other thoughts aside. Throughout her pregnancy, the notion of giving up her child made her so sad every time she thought about it that she refused to acknowledge it. The closer the time came, however, the more sadness and dread built in the back of her mind like an avalanche of emotions waiting to fall at once.

A few minutes later, Elsie and the girls returned.

"Take my hand and squeeze it," Rose said as Libby began to restlessly fidget under the pain of a contraction. The clock on the wall indicated that she'd been in the hospital for almost four hours, but it seemed like only a few minutes. Rose glanced at her gold watch bracelet. "The contractions are only about three minutes apart now. I can't wait to find out whether it's a girl or a boy."

The girls all agreed to wait until birth to find out the gender of their babies beforehand, deciding to be surprised once the children were delivered. Libby had the distinct feeling her child was a girl and confided her hunch to Rose but didn't tell anyone else.

"I don't think I could handle this by myself," Rachel said to Lindsay. "I'm so glad you're here with me." She stared at Libby and Rose. "You girls, too. I'm going to miss all of you when we go our separate ways."

"Who says we need to split up?" Lindsay countered. "We can still keep in touch with each other wherever we go. Right?"

"I'd like that very much," Libby admitted. "You know, in the beginning, I didn't want to stay at Elsie's farm. It felt like I was being sequestered against my will to keep from embarrassing my dad. I don't know who recommended her, but I'm so glad now that my dad listened to that person. Otherwise, I would never have met any of you. You are the sisters I never had."

"Me, too! Then, it's settled," Rose declared. "I volunteer to keep track of everyone's addresses and phone numbers so none of us get out of touch." They gave each other a high-five and laughed, enjoying the only light moment of their day so far.

Throughout the afternoon, the nurse made multiple visits to examine Rachel as her contractions grew closer together. In late afternoon, the nurse returned with a tall, lanky young man clad in light blue scrubs. "Pray for me!" Rachel cried, as though she feared the worst.

The girls watched somberly as they wheeled Rachel out of the room.

The girls bowed their heads and said a prayer for Rachel and her baby.

"It won't be long now," Rose said checking her watch again, obviously to steer her mind from Rachel's predicament. "Concentrate on your breathing, you're doing fine."

Rose is a great coach, Libby thought, letting her mind wander, *but Cash should be here now. It's his child. His responsibility! He has no idea what he's put me through, but if I ever see him again, I'm going to—*

She didn't get a chance to finish the thought. A severe contraction shot twisting pain across her lower back and down her thighs, making her forget all about him.

At approximately five o' clock, Libby delivered a healthy, seven-pound, four-ounce baby girl. The nurse took the child away soon after her birth, but Libby got a glimpse of her baby before the tiny bundle disappeared from the room and her life. After the staff finished up and left, she lay quietly, fighting the urge to cry.

I want to see my baby, she thought as a tear fell from the corner of her eye. *I want to hold her. I don't want to give her up.*

The door opened. A female staff person rolled in a monitor. A male staff person in light blue scrubs wheeled Rachel's bed into the room. Her eyes were closed, and her motionless body lay hooked up to an IV bag. The man pulled the curtain closed to attend to her in private, but Libby heard the unmistakable sound of the heart machine as he hooked her up to the monitor.

After the hospital staff left, Elsie and the girls quietly entered. Lindsay went behind the curtain to see Rachel. Elsie and Rose stayed with Libby.

"Visiting hours are almost up. We have to go," Elsie said quietly as she patted Libby's cheek. "Rachel needs time to recover, and you need to rest too." She straightened Libby's covers and then looked up. "Do you want anything before we go? A soda or a snack?"

Libby shook her head. "I have ice water." She glanced toward the curtain separating her from Rachel. "Is Rachel going to be okay?"

Elsie winced at the sound of her question. "They had to take the baby by C-section," she whispered slowly. "It was a boy."

The sad tone in her reply made Libby's heart flutter with dread. "Is he okay?"

Elsie shook her head and placed a finger to her lips to warn Libby against any more questions in case Rachel could hear them. She swallowed hard, staring at Elsie as she absorbed the news.

"We'll be back tomorrow, after the doctor releases you, to bring you home," she said and signaled to Rose to notify Lindsay that they needed to leave. Rose disappeared behind the curtain and reappeared with Lindsay. Both were somber looking after seeing Rachel.

After they left, Libby lay in the quiet of her room reliving her day, from the moment she felt her first contraction to the delivery of her baby.

I've got to see her, she thought desperately. *I need to see my baby before they take her away forever.*

Sitting up in bed, she eased slowly over the side, dropping her feet onto the cool floor. She tiptoed to the door and peered through a narrow crack. A young blonde woman sat behind the counter at the nurse's station speaking with a visitor. Libby didn't have any idea where the nursery was located but knew it had to be close by. And it was— across the corridor from her room. She gazed through the window and saw several bassinettes in the room, but only one appeared occupied. The one holding her baby.

Excited to see her child, she dashed into the room and peered into the bassinet. A tiny bundle wrapped in a pink blanket lay in the center, sleeping quietly. Exceedingly fine wisps of dark hair covered the top of her delicate head.

This is my baby, she thought in fascination. *This is my little girl.*

Suddenly, all that mattered to her was this child. Gazing down at the sleeping baby, she realized the enormous responsibility that came with becoming a parent and the emotions her own mother must have experienced the day she was born.

"I'm sorry, God," she whispered. "I take back everything I said about you, and I ask your forgiveness for all the things I've done wrong. To bless me with this precious life after the way I've treated you proves that you love me and you aren't holding my sins against me."

As usual, God didn't answer her, but her mood immediately lifted, as though a huge weight had lifted off her shoulders.

She checked the pink card inserted into a slot at the end of the bassinet. It read, 'Baby Girl, Cunningham.'

"How sad," she whispered to the sleeping child. "You don't even have a name." The child's adoptive family would name her, but until then, she would simply be "Baby Girl."

Fascinated, she pulled back the blanket and stared at the newborn's tiny frame. The child had a plastic ID bracelet fastened around her ankle and another one around her wrist. Making a split-second decision, Libby pulled the ankle bracelet apart and stuffed it inside the thick bun she'd wound her hair into at the top of her head. If anyone caught her in here, they wouldn't find the bracelet and ask her what she was doing with it. She quickly wrapped the baby back in her blanket and left the room, closing the door quietly behind her.

Tomorrow, she thought as she slid back into bed, *when the hospital is full of people and no one is paying attention to me, I'll sneak out of here and visit my baby again. I just want to hold my child...*

*   *   *

The next morning the ringing of the phone woke her. Half-asleep, she leaned over and picked up the handset off the small cabinet between the two beds. "Hello?"

"Libby!" The familiar voice sounded cheerful. "It's Barbara. Did I wake you?"

"Not really," she whispered groggily. "I had breakfast at seven. I was just resting my eyes for a little bit." More awake now, she raised the head of her bed to sit up. "How are you? How is Uncle Bob and Medley?"

"We're all fine here. I called to find out how *you're* doing," Barbara replied with a note of concern in her words. "You and the little one."

"I'm doing okay. I had a little girl. I planned to call you today and let you know. How did you find out?"

"Elsie called me as soon as you went into labor," Barbara said matter-of-factly. "She kept in touch throughout the day."

Oh, right, Libby thought. Aunt Barbara and Elsie really hit it off at the family event last month. She wondered if they had chatted at times other than yesterday. Probably so. Medley knew how upset Libby was about Cash when they left after the party, and Barbara had probably called later to get updates from Elsie.

"How is Dad? Does he know?"

"Not yet," Barbara said, sounding frustrated. "I called his office, but his staff said he's out for the next seven days, so I imagine he's on a confidential trip somewhere. I left a message with them to have him call me back. If he's overseas, it might take him a while to get back to me, but I stressed to his assistant that I needed to urgently speak with him. For all the good it will do..." She paused momentarily. "Anyway, I haven't said anything to Mother. I'm going to let Frank handle that duty himself."

Libby's heart fell. The one person she really wanted to speak with about the baby was her father, but as usual, his job got in the way of his personal life. "Well, when he comes back into the country, he'll probably call me."

"Has Frank spoken to you about going back to school?" Barbara asked.

That seemed an odd question to be asked at a time like this. "No," Libby replied. "All I know is that I'm staying with Elsie until Lindsay and Rose have their babies. Then all four of us girls are leaving together. Why, did Dad say something to you about it?"

Barbara sighed. "Only that he's been looking at a private school in Seattle. How do you feel about that?"

It sounds about right to me, Libby thought pessimistically. *It's about as far away from here as I can get.*

"The next time you talk to him, tell him I agree," she said. "I'm fine with going to school in Seattle but I want a debit card and in return, I promise not to flunk any classes or get myself kicked out."

Barbara paused again, as though surprised by her straightforward answer. "All right, I'll be sure to relay the message for you."

She and Barbara talked a little while longer but before she hung up, she asked her aunt to say hi to Medley when she arrived home. Her cousin, apparently, was spending MEA weekend at a museum tour in Chicago.

"How are you feeling today?" Libby asked Rachel as she put the handset back on the base.

Rachel lay on her bed, pale and worn. Her short, dark hair needed a good brushing. "I'm tired," she replied listlessly. "How about you?"

Libby fell back against her bed and threw her arm over her eyes. "Yes! I'd give anything for a double latte right now." Elsie had a fancy coffee bar that made espresso, latte, and cappuccino.

"Me, too," Rachel replied. "There's nothing like that here. Just weak coffee with artificial creamer. I guess we'll have to wait until we get home for the premium stuff." She glanced at Libby. "You're lucky. You get to go home today. The doctor said I need to stay for a couple of days."

"I'm sorry about your baby," Libby said solemnly, deciding to address the issue rather than ignore it.

Rachel didn't answer right away. She lay in bed staring at the ceiling, filling the moment with an awkward silence. "He had a heart defect," she said at last. "I—I..." Her eyes filled with tears. She wiped them away with the back of her hands. "I heard you talking to your aunt," she said, quickly changing the subject. "So, you're going to Seattle when you leave Elsie's?"

"My dad has been looking into a school there," Libby replied slowly then she shrugged. "It really doesn't matter where I go as long as I don't have to go back home and live with my grandmother. I used to be desperate to live with her and my dad, but she doesn't want me there and he's never home, so I'm ready to be on my own again."

Rachel raised her bed and adjusted her position, grimacing from the pain of her incision. "You've changed a lot since you first came to the farm," she said after a long, painful sigh. "The first day we met, you were so nervous and unhappy that I remember wondering if you were going to make it."

I remember wondering the same thing about you, Libby thought.

"Your identity was wrapped up in your boyfriend and he was all you ever talked about." Rachel grabbed a large Styrofoam cup of ice water off her tray table and took a sip. "I was like that for a long time, too, but Lindsay made me see that the guy I had counted on wasn't going to miraculously bail me out of my predicament. I had to work through it myself."

"She told me pretty much the same thing," Libby replied with a sigh. "That's when I finally admitted to myself that no one cared enough to help me make things right—not my family nor my ex-boyfriend. I was my own."

The door to their room suddenly opened and the doctor, an elderly white-haired gentleman walked in wearing a white lab coat over his dark suit. "Good morning," he said amicably to both girls. He pulled the curtain around Rachel's bed. "Let's take a look at your incision."

Now that she was alone, Libby quietly slipped into the busy hallway and walked across to the nursery. No one told her she couldn't see her child, but no one asked her if she wanted to see the baby before they took her away either. Determined to see her newborn one more time, she went in and gazed with fascination at the sleeping bundle in the bassinet. The child's fine cap of dark hair reminded her of Cash. Sadly, he'd never know how much she'd inherited from him.

The baby stirred, making soft noises.

She's absolutely perfect. Thank you, God, for giving her life, Libby thought. Completely enamored with the new person she and Cash had created, she pulled back the blanket and took the child's tiny hand in hers. She smiled to herself. *You made something good out of a bad mistake, God. I wish I could take her home with me.*

But where was home? Even if she had convinced her dad to let her keep the baby, then what? Where did she belong? Not with him and Grandma Norma. Who then? Aunt Barbara and Uncle Bob? Even if she begged her aunt and uncle to take her in, she couldn't see them consenting to take on the added responsibility. A pregnant teen was one thing, but a teen with a newborn was a lot for them to handle at this stage in their lives.

A still, small voice warned her not to, but she ignored the voice

149

of reason in her head and lifted the bundle out of the bassinet to hold the baby in her arms. Just for a minute. It felt so natural, so right to cradle her. Looking into the child's sweet little face, her heart swelled with love. Deep in her heart, she knew it was wrong to surrender her precious baby for someone else to raise. They were meant to be together. Her eyes filled with desperate tears.

Knowing what I know now, how can I give her up? God, please help me. I can't do this!

The door suddenly opened and a slim woman with short brown hair walked in wearing a green uniform, pulling a mop and bucket on wheels. Her eyes widened when she saw Libby holding the baby.

Libby froze, clutching her child in her arms.

The woman smiled kindly as she pushed the bucket inside the room and shut the door. Her name tag read Renee, Housekeeping. "Hi, there. How are you?"

"Fine," Libby managed to say.

"What a sweet baby," Renee remarked as she smiled down at the sleeping child. "What's her name?"

Uncomfortable, Libby gazed down at her little girl. "She—she doesn't have one yet."

The softening in Renee's golden-brown eyes revealed that she understood what Libby meant. She'd guessed that Libby was one of the temporary residents at Elsie Peterson's farm and was surrendering the child.

"Say," Renee said kindly, "we keep an instant camera at the nurse's station to take pictures of kids when they stay here. Why don't I fetch it and get a picture of you holding your little one? Would you like that?"

Libby's jaw dropped. "You'd do that for me?"

"Of course," Renee said enthusiastically and pushed her mop bucket to the side. "I'll be right back."

Renee left the room but returned quickly, as she'd promised. "Why don't you stand in front of the bassinet so I can get a good shot? You're right under the light. Now smile!"

Libby's smile came effortlessly, knowing in her heart that she'd never been happier in her life. She watched Renee snap the picture and pull the image from the camera—just a black square at first. Renee handed the shot to Libby and together they watched the image form before their eyes.

"Aw," Renee cooed once the picture fully developed. "It's perfect." She held up the camera. "I'd better get this back to the nurse's station so I can get this room cleaned."

"Thank you!" Libby barely got the words out before Renee left the room. She set the baby back in the bassinet and pulled open a small drawer, hoping to find something to hold the picture. Someone had placed a small baggie with cotton balls in the drawer along with other items of necessity. Libby opened the little bag and stuffed the picture into it along with various items in the drawer, including one of the pink identification cards on the bassinet. She wanted these things as a remembrance of this day.

She returned to her room with the baggie and a new idea, but she needed to talk to Elsie first.

*   *   *

Elsie and the girls arrived at noon, just as Libby and Rachel were finishing up their lunch. Lindsay and Rose went straight to Rachel to check on how she was feeling.

"I spoke to Amanda, the nurse on duty. She told me that Dr. Benson has released you," Elsie said to Libby. She wore chocolate brown corduroy jeans today and a cream turtleneck under a brown, hip-length sweater. She checked her watch. "Ready to go?"

Libby slid off the edge of the bed. "Can I talk to you about something first?"

Elsie's eyebrows furrowed in puzzlement. "All right. Let's go into the hallway." They left the room and shut the door. "What's this all about? Is something wrong?"

Libby glanced around to make sure no one else was listening. "I've changed my mind. I want to keep the baby. And—and...I want to live with you."

Elsie's eyes widened in surprise. "Oh, honey, I'm afraid that's not possible."

Libby's heart dropped to the floor. "Why not? You have a big house, and I won't be any trouble. I promise!"

"I know you wouldn't," Elsie replied in a soft voice. "That's not the problem. It's just that...they came for the baby an hour ago. She's in transit to a foster home in the Twin Cities right now to await placement."

"She's gone?" Libby's heart began to hammer uncontrollably. "But—I just saw her a while ago. She can't be—"

She rushed into the nursery and to her horror, all the bassinettes were empty. The one her baby had lain in had been stripped of everything—blankets, accessories, and the remaining pink card that identified her. Could it really have been that long since she'd held her child? It felt like only ten minutes had passed.

Elsie followed her into the nursery and put her arms around Libby. "I'm so sorry, Libby. I know what you're going through."

"How can you," Libby mumbled through her tears. "You've never..." She looked up and saw the truth in Elsie's deep blue eyes. "You did, didn't you?"

"Yes," Elsie replied, her eyes becoming misty. "I was about your age when it happened. The boy abandoned me and left me to struggle with the difficulty of dealing with it on my own. I had no one to turn to for help, especially when my mother threatened to disown me unless I gave up my child."

Everything suddenly began to make sense: Elsie's willingness to take in pregnant girls, her warmth and understanding. "What happened to your baby?" Libby blurted. "Did you ever get to see her again? How old is your kid now?"

"I did find her, but it was too late," Elsie said with a sniffle. "She died of leukemia at five years old. Her adoptive parents sent a letter to me by way of the adoption agency after she passed away."

Libby slid her arms around Elsie and hugged her tightly. "Elsie, I'm so sorry."

"I'm sorry for your loss, too," Elsie said gravely and hugged Libby back.

"I love you, Elsie," Libby said as she wiped a tear with the back of her hand. Never once had she uttered those words to either her grandmother or her dad but now, it seemed effortless to tell her temporary guardian. Someone she'd only known for a few short months, but who had become the mother she'd never had.

"I love you too, honey," Elsie said in a thick voice. "Come on. Let's go home. You're going to be okay."

Libby smiled through her tears, grateful to have this woman in her life.

Chapter Sixteen

The next day…

"Where are you going?" Maggie stood at the kitchen counter with a wooden spoon in her hand, stirring beans in a crockpot. "Supper is ready."

"I won't be long. I'm going out to the garage," Cash said as he sauntered toward the back door. "I need to check the fluids in my car."

She tapped the spoon against the rim and set it in a spoon holder. "Well, don't leave the yard. We're going to eat as soon as your father gets home."

"No problem, Ma. I'm starving." Cash leisurely walked outdoors, taking in one of the last warm days of fall, and got as far as the garage door before he realized he'd left his keys in the house. On his way back, the phone rang in the kitchen.

"Hello?" Maggie asked briskly, sounding irritated at having her supper preparations interrupted. "Oh, hello." Her voice immediately changed to a serious tone. "No, this isn't a bad time. What can I do for you, Mr. Cunningham?"

The kitchen door shut abruptly. The lock made a distinct *click* as she turned it.

Cash stood at the bottom of the steps wondering what was going on between his mother and the senator. Oddly enough, he could still hear her voice clearly. He walked past the stairs and rounded the corner of the house to check the kitchen window. Yes, she'd left it open, not realizing how easily anyone could hear every word of her conversation. Curious, he stood under the window and leaned his back against the house with his arms folded as he listened.

"Oh, she did? Uh-huh," Maggie said, her words sounding more like a statement than a question. "Was the child born healthy? No complications for the mother? That's good."

Libby had the baby, Cash thought as his heart began to pound. *When? Where? Can I see the child?* He had so many questions.

"Is she going to keep the baby?" A pregnant pause. "Yes, well, given her young age, I guess that is the best solution for her and her daughter." Though she probably didn't realize it, the sadness in her voice gave away her disappointment. "Do you have a family lined up for the adoption?"

Cash nearly swallowed his tongue. *She's putting the baby up for adoption? Our little girl? Why? This isn't fair*, he thought, becoming angry. *First, they tell me I can't see her any longer, then they threaten me with retaliation if I do. Now they're deciding the fate of my child. I'm the father! Why are they shutting me out? I have rights!*

"Say that again?"

The sudden, almost shrill tone of surprise in Maggie's voice cut into Cash's thoughts, pulling his attention back to the conversation.

"That's very generous of you, Mr. Cunningham," Maggie said, sounding surprised, "but we're not asking for anything in return for agreeing not to file a paternity suit." She paused. "No strings attached? For his college education? But ten thousand dollars! That's a lot of money!"

Shocked, Cash shoved himself away from the house and turned, staring up at the window. Did he hear that right? The senator was gifting him ten thousand dollars for his education because he'd already agreed to keep quiet about the baby? A bribe dressed up as an unselfish act— that's all it was.

"Yes, we'll be home tonight," Maggie stated. "What time will your men stop by with the check?" She paused. "How about seven-thirty? All right then. We'll be expecting them. Goodbye."

Cash walked back to the steps and sat down, his mind in a daze. He had so much to process.

I'm a father, he thought numbly. *I have a daughter.* The thought fascinated him and yet the very idea frightened him at the same time. Having a child of his own was a mind-blowing thought.

His fragile elation quickly soured. "Yeah," he said aloud with a snort. "A daughter that I'll never know because I'm not allowed to acknowledge her." All because one powerful man stood between him and the two women he loved.

He sat on the step with his chin resting on the heel of his hand, staring at the ground as a wave of hopelessness shrouded his heart. He hadn't cried since his dog, Pedro, died when he was ten years old, but a rush of emotion suddenly clouded his eyes. How could such joyous, life-altering news make him so sad?

Because all the joy has been taken away.

He sat for a little while, staring at the ground, absorbing this life-altering news and feeling a profound sense of loss at losing his family.

But wait…

He distinctly heard Maggie say that the money had no strings attached. The senator's goons were dropping off a check. *For him.* That meant, to him, that he had the power to do whatever he wanted with it. Sure, he could use some of it for college, but he had another idea in mind. One that would put the money to better use.

"I'll hire the best lawyer I can find," he whispered to himself as he wiped away a tear using his sleeve. "Tell him the entire story and put together a plan to find my child."

He had no idea how his parents would receive the idea, but it didn't matter. He was eighteen now and in control of his own life. As soon as he accepted the senator's money, he'd have total control over that too. The irony almost made him laugh.

"I don't care if it takes the entire ten grand, and more. I'm going to legally adopt her," he said aloud as his father's car pulled into the driveway and the garage door ambled upward. Cash stood up and wiped his tear-stained hands on his T-shirt, ready to take on the world if need be. "The senator took Libby away from me, but he can't keep me away from my child."

He shoved his hands into his pockets and stared at the ground, his heart aching for the only woman he'd ever loved. The woman he *still* loved. He couldn't understand how she could give her child away—his child, but now that he knew about it, all was not lost. The baby would at least have one of her natural parents.

I'll fight for my little girl as long as it takes, he thought, with a new sense of purpose as the words developed a stronghold in his heart. *No one is ever going to take my daughter from me again.*

Part Three

A new beginning…

Chapter Seventeen

Monday, January 2nd

Libby climbed out of Elsie's SUV at the busy drop-off area of the Minneapolis/St. Paul International Airport, ready to begin a new phase of her life. The multi-lane drive-through held so many cars, that it resembled a slow-moving traffic jam. Huge Christmas wreaths decorated with red velvet bows hung next to each entrance. Multi-colored lights strung across the covered pedestrian bridge linking the buildings lit up the one-block area with a festive glow.

Elsie slipped out of the driver's seat and walked to the back of the vehicle. She reached into the open hatch and began to pull out the suitcases for all the girls. Senator Cunningham had offered to hire a limo to bring the girls to the airport, but everyone wanted Elsie to see them off, and they opted to use her car instead.

Each girl had a different flight destination, but because they'd booked morning flights, their departures were close together. Libby's eleven o'clock flight was the latest, giving her extra time to spend with Medley, Barbara, and Bob.

"Call me when you get to Seattle and let me know that you've arrived safely at the school," Elsie said as she hugged Libby one last time. "Frank has arranged a limo to pick you up at the airport and take you there."

A lump formed in Libby's throat. She and the girls had decided to stay at Elsie's over Christmas and be together through the holidays. They'd decorated her house to the hilt with lights, garland, and a seven-foot spruce tree and filled her kitchen with lots of baked goodies. It had turned out to be the best holiday she'd ever had. Living with Elsie had made a huge difference in her life. Both she and her companions would miss the woman terribly. "I will. I promise."

The girls stood at the curb and waved goodbye to Elsie as she drove away. They hauled their bags into the main area of the airport and immediately headed to the nearest coffee shop to get lattes before getting in line to get checked in. Once they got through the coffee line, it was time to go their separate ways.

Rose engulfed Libby with outstretched arms. "Give me a hug, Sugah! You keep in touch, ya hear?"

"Of course I will!"

Libby hugged Lindsay and Rachel as well, reminding each one of their group's promise to meet up again someday for a reunion.

After a tearful goodbye, she sipped on her latte as she wheeled her bag to the elevator. She'd arranged to meet the Grants at the coffee shop on the baggage level for a morning snack before their final goodbye.

They were already there, sitting at a table drinking coffee when she arrived.

"Hey!" Libby cried with outstretched arms as she approached them. Setting her latte on the table, she hugged each one in turn and then sat down to enjoy their company.

"We brought your favorite coffee cake," Medley said as she opened a Tupperware container filled with pieces of freshly baked cinnamon crunch cake.

"Yum! I need something to eat before I get on the plane, and this hits the spot! Thank you!"

"You must have had a great Christmas. Your face is glowing," Barbara said and leaned close, sliding her arm around Libby's shoulders. "I've never seen you so happy."

"The time I spent at Elsie's farm was the best months of my life," Libby replied truthfully. "I loved it there. I really did."

"How do you feel about going to school in Seattle?" Medley asked, looking a bit sad that her cousin was going to live so far away again. "It's not like you can drop by whenever you want."

Libby sat back in her chair, taking in the question. Six months ago, she would have been an emotional wreck at the prospect of going back to a private school. Now, she didn't mind the idea at all. The farther she moved away from places that reminded her of Cash, the better. "I'll be okay. I think it will be a good experience for me. I need a fresh start and moving to a new school in another state is the right approach."

Libby watched Bob and Barbara exchange curious glances, knowing they were amazed at how much she had changed. The Libby they knew before she went to live at Elsie's farm had been defiant, immature, and extremely unhappy. The Libby they saw now projected calm, self-reliance, and a positive outlook. Seven months in a loving, nurturing environment had made the difference. Love and gratitude for Elsie would always fill her heart.

"I'm looking forward to hanging out with you during the holidays and next summer," Medley said and sipped her coffee. "We never got to spend a day at the beach like we planned!"

"That would be great," Libby exclaimed. "I miss the fun we had last year at school!"

Barbara patted her hand. "You have a permanent invitation to stay with us."

"Thank you, Auntie Barbara. I would love to stay with you and

Uncle Bob," Libby said, determined that she would never go back to her father's house and suffer under Grandma Norma's harsh scrutiny. "By the way, do you have my debit card?"

"Yes, I do!" Barbara reached into her purse and pulled out a small bundle of papers. "I'm glad you reminded me. Here is your debit card, your reservation for the limo, and the documents you need for school."

Libby stuffed the items into her new purse and set it on her lap. Frank had given her a generous cash gift for Christmas to buy whatever she wanted. She chose to buy gifts for Elsie and the girls with it. Now that she had her new debit card, she'd use it to get new clothes for school.

They spent their last minutes together sipping steamy beverages and munching on Barbara's moist breakfast cake garnished with a toasted cinnamon/brown sugar topping. When it was time for Libby to leave, she hugged everyone and said her goodbyes.

"Take care of yourself, honey," Barbara whispered in a teary voice. "I love you."

"I love you too, Auntie. I'll call you when I get there and tell you all about my school."

Ninety minutes later Libby sat in a window seat in first class, watching the plane lift off the tarmac and ascend into the cloudless, azure sky as she munched on peanuts and a chilled glass of Coke. Somewhere in the city below, Cash was most likely at work or school, getting on with his life—without her.

She sipped on her Coke, wondering why he'd deserted her. Most likely, she'd never learn the truth, but it didn't matter. They'd gone their separate ways, the baby had been welcomed into a new family, and that was that.

What's done is done, she thought firmly. *I've made peace with God and forgiven Cash for abandoning me. I only hope he forgives me for giving up our child.*

Deep in her heart, though, she still loved him. The passage of time and a new boyfriend someday would probably make the yearning go away, but for now, it burned like a steady flame.

That day in the nursery flashed through her mind, causing a rush of melancholy to overtake her. She could still remember the exhilaration of holding her daughter in her arms. Of kissing the child's forehead and inhaling her sweet baby scent.

I love you, little one, she thought as she gazed at the clear blue sky, *and I always will. You're the light of my life, but you belong to someone else now. That doesn't mean I'll ever forget you, though. You'll never be far from my thoughts because you'll always be in my heart. One day, we'll meet again. I promise you. I'll never give up hope until I do.*

Sitting back in her wide, comfortable seat, she closed her eyes and exhaled a tired sigh. She didn't have a clue as to how she'd find her child or when, but she had hope.

And for now, that was enough.

The End

(For now, but not forever!)

Yes, things look bad, but *please* don't give up on Libby and Cash. Their story continues in book two, ***This Time Forever***, and I promise it has a happy ending! I've included the first chapter for you. Read on!

Denise Devine

This Time Forever

Denise Devine

USA Today Bestselling Author

This Time Forever

Book Two – Forever Yours Series

Does time really heal all wounds?

Libby Cunningham has finally found the daughter her father forced her to give up for adoption nearly sixteen years ago.

She has never forgiven herself and now desperately wants to make it up to Amber for the years they've lost. However, she has also learned that Cash MacKenzie, Amber's father, has custody. Libby has never forgotten that Cash broke her teenage heart and deserted her when she needed him the most. Now he holds the key to her future happiness. Can she overcome her memories of the past or will her feelings jeopardize the present?

From Cash's viewpoint, Libby couldn't have picked a worse time to intrude upon their lives.

Amber's rebellious attitude reminds him of Libby at that age. He doesn't need interference from the woman who abandoned her own child and realizes he's never forgiven her. What guarantee does he have that Libby won't walk away from Amber a second time? Libby's feelings for Amber may be genuine, but he will never allow her to hurt Amber—or him—ever again.

Chapter 1

Libby Cunningham had risked heartbreak in the past, but not like this. Never before had she come so close to finding the child her father forced her to give up for adoption almost sixteen years ago. Years spent praying and trusting God for a breakthrough had led to disappointment again and again—but not tonight. This time her heart possessed an unexplainable peace, giving her renewed hope. Had God finally answered her plea?

Then she saw the girl.

"That can't be my daughter," Libby murmured as she watched a teenager ascend the stairs of a crowded bleacher at the River's Edge High football game. "That young lady has someone else's genes."

Medley Grant reached over and squeezed her hand. "Lib, Lib, you've got to keep an open mind. I warned you that Amber might not be what you expected."

The crowd roared and Amber MacKenzie pivoted, gazing down at the play in progress. Towering floodlights cast a silvery sheen upon the tall, slender girl wearing a coral sweater and hip-hugging jeans. Waist-length hair hugged her shoulders and arms like a luxurious black shawl.

Libby studied every detail of the girl that she could glean from a distance, desperate to find some connection. "I expected to see something of myself in her," she confessed. Instead, she'd come to a dead end, once again facing the reality that the odds of finding her daughter didn't lean in her favor. "She doesn't resemble me at all."

"Yes, she does!" Medley looked up and stared at the girl, perusing Amber with a smile of approval. "She reminds me precisely of you at that age."

On the field, River's Edge cheerleaders led the raucous crowd into a frenzy of school spirit. Clad in maroon skirts and gold sweaters, they swung matching pom-poms and kicked their legs high. "Push 'em back, push 'em back, w-a-y-y-y back! G-o-o-o Otters!" Behind them, both teams joined arms in their respective huddles, discussing their next plays.

Libby ignored the game and the crush of boisterous spectators seated elbow to elbow on the hard, metal bleachers. The crisp September evening provided perfect weather for football, but she and her cousin never intended to spend their time watching the game. They were here on a mission—to find Amber MacKenzie. Ever since the girl walked into Medley's salon last week to get a trim, Medley had pressured Libby to attend this event and observe Amber for herself.

Libby twisted at the waist, her gaze sliding from Amber back to her cousin. "What do you see that I don't? I'm blonde and fair. She's so...totally like her father."

Medley paused, holding a couple of kernels of popcorn to her burgundy-tinted lips. "She inherited Cash MacKenzie's looks, but I see other ways you two are exactly alike. That day she came into the salon, I noticed aspects about her that reminded me of you. She has your tall, slender frame. You both frown the same way when you're reading. Oh, and another thing," Medley paused to sip her soda, "Amber's voice..." Medley's fine, penciled brows arched. "She sounds exactly like you."

"I wish I knew for sure." Libby sighed and looked away, not

wanting Medley to see her doubt. A couple of similar attributes didn't prove a thing. "If she's almost sixteen she could be mine. If she's younger, then she's his daughter by someone else."

Even though it happened long ago, the thought of Cash MacKenzie marrying so soon after he'd severed all ties with her still touched a nerve. How could he have forgotten her so easily? Had he been seeing someone else all along? That could explain why he'd turned his back on her when she needed him the most...

She stared hard at Amber, wishing with all her heart this girl could be *the one*. For a moment, she dared to entertain the possibility.

"All these years I've believed total strangers adopted my baby," she declared. "If Amber *is* my child and her biological father raised her..." Libby's throat tightened as a simple question hovered in her mind. How did Cash end up with Amber? The only answer possible proved difficult to bear. The people closest to her, the ones she'd trusted, had deceived her.

Amber reached the top row. Squeezing past several people, she slowly made her way to her seat.

"There's Cash." Medley nudged Libby in the ribs. "Wow. The years have been good to him, haven't they?"

The mere mention of his name made Libby tense. Ignoring the comment, she focused straight ahead and pretended to watch the game, but the players on the field quickly melded into a blur as the ploy failed and painful memories ambushed her. The past clouded her thoughts as she recalled the wayward, motherless girl of sixteen who thought she'd grasped the chance to have everything she'd ever wanted—the love of her life and a family of her own. Instead, she'd ended up lonely and alone, rejected by Cash MacKenzie, the only man she'd ever loved or trusted. She didn't want to glance in his direction much less take inventory of his seasoned good looks. It took years to get over him, even longer to forgive him for what he'd done—and left undone.

171

Medley's gentle nudge brought Libby's attention back to the present. She expelled an unhappy sigh. "What's *he* doing here? You said Amber planned to come with a friend."

"That's what Amber told me," Medley chirped in her bird-like voice. She looked like a nosegay of fall chrysanthemums in her gold Ann Taylor sweater and dark green slacks. Her chin-length flip of auburn hair glistened with burgundy highlights. "Maybe her friend canceled."

Libby cut Medley a sidewise glance. "Or maybe you secretly arranged this little reunion."

"Don't be ridiculous!" Medley's quick laugh pierced the air. "When have I ever tried to match you up with a man?" Her heavy lashes fluttered. "Well, not this time. Honestly, I didn't know he'd be here." She leaned close. "But I did Google him on the Internet the other day." A mischievous smile turned up the corners of her full lips. "He's not married, you know."

"Cash MacKenzie's personal life is of no interest to me." Libby pointed a warning finger at her. "So, don't even *think* of hatching a scheme to get us together!"

"Aren't you even curious about him?" Medley gazed up at Cash like an adoring groupie. "Like I said, he's still a hunk." She held out a small set of binoculars. "See for yourself."

Libby pushed the binoculars away. "No thanks." Medley's cheerful persistence grated on her nerves, but her cousin had no way of knowing how deeply Cash had wounded her. She didn't see any purpose in discussing the unpleasant details of her past, so she let it go.

"What about Amber?" Medley's jade eyes twinkled. "You've waited so long. Don't you want to gaze upon your own daughter? You'll adore her once you meet her."

"Meet her?" Libby shot her cousin an annoyed look. "On what basis? I have absolutely no proof she's my child."

"She *is* your daughter. I knew it the moment I saw her." Medley grabbed Libby's hand and slapped the binoculars into her palm. "Here. Satisfy your curiosity, once and for all."

Libby debated only a moment. Then she gingerly tugged on the visor of her maroon and gold cap and leaned back to see past the shoulders of the mountainous man sitting to her right. She lifted the silver, palm-sized spyglasses and peered into the stands.

Amber MacKenzie sat tall and straight like a porcelain doll. Heavy lashes hooded her cocoa eyes as she scanned the crowd instead of watching the game. Nothing in either the girl's manner or her features convinced Libby they were mother and daughter.

Someone bumped her elbow, shifting the binoculars sharply to the left. Her hand froze as a tall, broad-shouldered man wearing jeans and a long-sleeved denim shirt popped into view. The front hung open, revealing a gold T-shirt stretched across a wide, muscular chest. Cash MacKenzie, the man who'd shattered her teenage heart looked exactly as she remembered him, only more handsome and more mature. A little voice in the back of her mind warned her to look away, but curiosity held her. At thirty-five, he still had thick, onyx hair. His dark eyes still held the bold, piercing look of a man who planned to conquer the world but now reflected wisdom and confidence as well. He leaned toward his daughter and spoke into her ear. Amber responded with stony silence, her bow-shaped lips pursed into a defiant pout.

Cash kept his expression calm and appeared to accept the rejection, but Libby sensed his tension as he looked away.

The chill between father and daughter continued, vacillating between clipped words and taut silence. Libby watched for several minutes, caught up in the drama of their little family spat. Something in Amber's stubborn expression bothered Libby, giving her the unshakable feeling the girl's unhappiness ran deeper than mere teenage growing pains. She seemed troubled...

Libby sensed someone watching her. She shifted the binoculars and found herself staring straight into Cash's visual line of fire. For a moment she floundered, stunned as his dark, piercing gaze seared through her.

A scene flashed through her mind, sweeping her back to a sultry, starry night. Cash's sinewy arms encircled her waist, his lips softly brushing hers as he whispered, "I'll always love you..."

Liar!

A hollow feeling seeped through her, displacing her peace with emptiness, as though the bottom had just dropped out of her soul. She ducked her head and spun around, using the bulky man next to her as a shield.

Stop this nonsense, she chided herself, aware that her emotions were getting out of hand. *You don't love him anymore. You'd be crazy to love him still—after what he did to you!*

"I need popcorn," she blurted to get her mind off the subject and thrust her fingers into the red and white box, almost knocking it out of Medley's hands.

"Touchdown!" Coronets and drums blasted out the school song.

Medley sprang to her feet with the thundering crowd as they gave the team a standing ovation. Libby followed, using the distraction to keep her mind off the most unsettling moment she'd experienced in a long time. She snatched the popcorn box from Medley and stuffed a handful into her mouth. Did Cash recognize her? "I hope not," she worried aloud.

Medley cupped one ear with her hand. "What?"

"Nothing," Libby shouted over the cheering and clapping. "Nothing that—"

"What? Did you say 'who's that?' I don't know, but he sure is trying hard to get Amber's attention."

Medley motioned toward an attractive young man at the base of the bleachers, standing off to one side. The tall youth wore low-rise, faded jeans and, despite the cool evening, a rust-colored tank top that showed off his lean, muscular build. Thick, walnut brown hair hung in loose waves about his shoulders. Libby lifted the binoculars once again and watched him make signals with his thumb and forefinger. She shifted her focus to Amber, who discreetly signaled back.

The crowd returned to their seats. Libby sat down and observed the teenage instant messaging in progress, curious about the secret conversation. Were they simply flirting, or being cautious because Cash disapproved of their friendship? That could explain why they weren't exchanging text messages or why the boy didn't simply climb the bleachers to talk to her.

Loud booing swelled among the crowd. The man next to Libby jumped out of his seat and blocked her view as he shook his fist, loudly disagreeing with the ref's call. She turned back to the activity on the field, but her thoughts only intensified on Amber and the pain of not finding her child. Despair crept into her heart, draining her hope. Why bother to stay any longer when the answer seemed clear? She'd reached another dead-end.

Libby glanced into the stands and saw Cash sitting alone, talking on his cell phone. She nudged Medley. "Amber is gone. So is her...um...friend."

Medley scooped up her designer handbag. "Yeah," she responded in a tone that sounded more like a question. "I saw them sneak off together while you were daydreaming. Want to take a walk and get a closer look at her?"

Libby slung the strap of her purse over her shoulder and stood. "Amber MacKenzie's social life is none of my business." She checked the time on her cell phone, noting that she should be going over last-minute details of a pre-nuptial dinner scheduled for tomorrow night. Her

175

job as an event planner for a local restaurant didn't run itself. "Let's go. There's only a minute left of the fourth quarter and River's Edge is ahead by fourteen points." She looked up, scrutinizing Cash McKenzie once more. "This game is over."

They squeezed past a half-dozen people, made their way down the crowded stands, and headed toward the school parking lot.

Libby surveyed seemingly endless rows of vehicles. "Do you remember where we parked?"

Medley gestured toward the farthest corner. "Over there." However, once they reached *over there* they still couldn't find Medley's car.

"What's the deal here?" Gripping her hands on her almost non-existent hips, Medley stopped and looked around. "How hard can it be to find a blue Focus?"

They wandered through more rows, looking for Medley's car.

Medley suddenly grabbed Libby by the forearm. "Don't look now, but Amber and her friend are right over..." She nodded toward the driver's side of a red Grand Am. "...there."

Libby craned her neck to see them.

"Don't stare! You'll give us away!"

Curious, Libby looked anyway. Amber stood in a semi-circle with five other teens, sharing a cigarette. The boy in the rust-colored tank top stood next to her, his muscular arm draped possessively around her shoulders as he gazed intently into her eyes.

Libby knew that look. It meant trouble.

Suddenly Cash appeared out of nowhere and strode toward his daughter, his expression grim, hands clenched at his sides. He grasped her by the arm and pulled her away from the boy.

"The restrooms are over there," he said to Amber and pointed across the lot. "What are you doing here?"

Crimson, Amber glanced at the other teens. "I'm talking to my friends, Dad! Go away!" She tried to hide the cigarette behind her back, but Cash grabbed her hand and tossed the butt to the damp ground. He splayed her fingers, exposing a large class ring. Shaking his head, he slipped it off her hand.

"Don't!" Amber grabbed at it to get it back.

Cash held up the ring in the boy's face. "Is this yours?"

The teen reciprocated with an arrogant shrug.

"Take it back. She's too young for you."

"Stop it!" Tears pooled in Amber's eyes. "Leave Brian alone!"

Scowling, Brian snatched his ring back.

Cash rebounded with a stern look. "Smoking, ditching homework, skipping school—my daughter never did any of those things until she started hanging out with *you*."

Brian cut Amber a sideways glance then stared back at Cash. "If you say so."

Cash let the statement go unchallenged and turned his back to the group. "C'mon, we're going home," he said tersely to Amber. Their gazes locked—hers rife with defiance and resentment, his burdened with disappointment and pain.

As he turned to go, he glanced across the trunk of the car and met Libby's gaze. Jolting to a stop, he blinked and did a double-take, his mouth gaping as though he couldn't believe what he saw—or, more accurately, *whom*.

Libby froze, but her heart pounded so hard she feared everyone could hear it. She never meant for Cash to see her, much less realize that she'd witnessed the entire episode at his expense.

"Oh-oh. Time to go," Medley whispered.

Libby barely heard the words but knew she needed to get out of there. She needed to escape from *him,* a living reminder of the most tragic event of her life. Without a word, she turned and swiftly walked away, leaving Cash MacKenzie to stare after her.

*   *   *

Cash drove out of the parking lot in an emotional daze. His hands steered, his foot accelerated and worked the brakes, but his heart shifted his thoughts into instant replay mode, reviewing the scene back at school.

"You embarrassed me, Dad! You made me look stupid!"

He vaguely heard the sobbing accusation. It sounded like Amber, but thoughts churned in his mind so hard he couldn't concentrate on anything other than navigating his pickup.

"You look fine," he mumbled, barely aware he'd replied.

Libby...

He still couldn't believe it. Had their paths crossed accidentally, or had she deliberately planned this encounter?

Her tall, slender image loomed in his mind like a permanent screensaver in Technicolor. She looked the same, yet different. She still wore her blonde hair long and sleek. And she still looked good in jeans and a blue blazer—the color of her eyes. Yet, something about her made him pause. Besides the passage of time, what made her seem different? He stared at the road ahead, wondering why it mattered. After all, she had turned her back on him and Amber long ago. He thought the years had erased the hurt over the betrayal they'd suffered, but it still lived in his heart. He clutched his gut. Now it had affected his stomach, too.

"I'll never be able to face my friends again! Tomorrow everyone in school will be talking about me. And laughing!"

"We'll discuss it when we get home," he muttered.

178

So... Why show up now? What did Libby want? An accusing little voice whispering from a far corner of his mind suggested what he already suspected; she'd come back to reclaim her daughter. She meant to take Amber away from him. The possibility made his stomach burn like acid.

He reached into his shirt pocket and pulled out a roll of antacids, popping two into his mouth, and chewing them like candy. The pain in his stomach flared. He devoured two more. His stomach couldn't take any more bad news. Amber's obsessive crush on a kid with a bad attitude had him tied in knots. Libby Cunningham's intrusion could destroy his family.

What's going on, Lord? You've already pushed me into a season of testing with Amber. Do you expect me to deal with Libby Cunningham, too? Why are all of these things happening at once? What are you trying to do, turn me inside out?

"I'm never going to school again! Ever!"

Amber's shouting finally broke through his thoughts. He cut her a sideways glance. If she hugged the door any closer, she'd be in the street.

"You're the worst dad in the world," she spat with a loud sob. Tears streamed down her cheeks. "I hate you! I hate you! I'm going to run away!"

Cash turned into his driveway and shut off the engine. At any other time, he would have bridled at Amber's behavior and grounded her on the spot. Today, however, her tantrum seemed tame compared to what he'd just experienced. Gripping the steering wheel with one hand and clutching the keys—still in the ignition—with the other hand, he tipped his head back, closed his eyes, and expelled a deep groan. He had a bad feeling his life would never be the same again.

Suddenly, he became aware of an odd silence in the truck. Pushing aside his troubled thoughts, he looked sideways at Amber. She sat smeared to the door, glowering at him with the tenacity of a cornered wolverine.

"You haven't heard a word I've said!" She rounded out the claim with an exaggerated sniff and swiped the back of her hand across her cheek. Thick, wet lashes fringed her large brown eyes. It reminded him of how she looked as a young child. She had once been so sweet, so trusting, and carefree. He wanted his little girl back. Where had she gone?

Amber continued to stare at him as if his reticence garnered suspicion. "H-how come you're not yelling at me for smoking and sneaking off with Brian?"

He couldn't imagine how to explain what he'd just been through, so he stayed silent.

She sat up straight and placed her hand on the door latch, frowning in confusion. "What's the matter with you, Dad? Ever since we got into the truck, you've been acting strange. Spaced out—like you've been struck by lightning or something." She squinted, giving him a curious once-over, as though trying to catch something she'd previously missed. "Are you okay?"

Struck by lightning? Or the divine hand of God? Deep in his heart, Cash knew God had put him on notice today and the pain in his gut told him he'd better pay attention because neither Libby Cunningham nor his indigestion planned to go away. Or God, for that matter. But what God wanted from him he wouldn't give—couldn't give. All these years he'd believed he'd forgiven Libby for deserting him and their child. Seeing her today made him realize he'd neither forgiven nor forgotten what she'd done.

Man, did he have a mess on his hands. He had problems with Amber, Libby, and now, God, too. He reached into his pocket, hunting for his antacids. The way things were going, he figured he'd soon be buying them by the case.

*　　*　　*

"I know you meant well, Medley, but we've checked her out and she's not my daughter. So, let's put it behind us and move on. Okay?" Libby paced the ivory carpet of Medley's living room, making a futile attempt to walk off her frustration.

Medley emerged from the kitchen with two orange mugs of French roast and set them on the coffee table next to a tin of chocolate-dipped biscotti. She collapsed onto her white leather sofa with a satisfied sigh and kicked off her dark green shoes. "Sit down, Libby." She patted the cushion next to her.

Medley's condominium looked like an IKEA showroom with leather furniture, glass, and wood bookcases, and brass table lamps, all in the modern, simplistic styling that described her outlook on nearly everything. "Let's have some Starbucks and discuss our next move."

Libby walked over to the window instead, lifted the curtain, and stared down at the tree-lined street. The burgeoning fall colors in Minneapolis provided a mosaic of scarlet, orange, and gold under the glow of city streetlights.

"I appreciate your wanting to help find my daughter, I really do, but we struck out this time and I don't see the point in talking about it anymore. We gave it our best shot. Unfortunately, it didn't turn out as we'd hoped it would." Her sigh formed a misty spot on the glass. "I'm tired and I have a busy day at work tomorrow. I need to go home."

Home meant the lonely, six-bedroom monstrosity overlooking Lake Harriet that she'd inherited from her late father, former U.S. Senator, Franklin Cunningham.

"What you really need is to lighten up." Medley pursed her lips as she pulled the cover off the tin. "You can't be tense when you talk to Cash; otherwise you may not be able to convince him that the best situation for Amber is to have both her parents involved in her life."

181

Libby let the curtain fall and spun away from the window. "Medley, I'm not going to put myself through embarrassing agony and call him begging for non-existent information." The stress of another defeat had taken its toll. She swallowed hard, fighting a catch in her throat. "Didn't you notice when they were arguing how much alike they looked? It's obvious she's not mine!"

"Of course, she is!" Medley's quick smile asserted that she believed it without a doubt.

"How can you be so sure? She doesn't possess a single characteristic that resembles me."

"Lib, Lib, you're just upset because so much is at stake. It's natural to be apprehensive." Medley offered her a steaming mug. "You've dreamed of this moment for years."

Libby walked back to the sofa and sat down. She accepted the coffee and took a sip. The rich, hot liquid soothed her throat but did nothing for her morale.

"Cash didn't appreciate our intrusion. We both saw the shock on his face. Even if, by a remote chance, Amber is my daughter, I can't imagine him welcoming me into her life."

"He knows what's best for her. He'll do the right thing." Medley set her mug on the coffee table. "You want to know the truth, don't you? So, you can put this behind you and get on with your life?"

"You know I do."

Medley picked up her cell phone and placed it in Libby's free hand. "Then stop being so stubborn about this. Swallow your doubts and make the call. For Amber's sake as well as your own, confront him and get it over with."

Libby's hand shook so hard she could barely set her mug down. She held the gold bling case in her quaking palm and stared at it as unbearable pain filled her heart. She dreaded the thought of having her hopes destroyed again—like so many times in the past. Now that she had observed Amber, the mirror image of Cash MacKenzie, would today be any different?

Medley produced a business card from her handbag. "He owns a construction company. Amber dug this out of her backpack when I said I wanted to remodel the kitchen." She placed it on the coffee table and pushed it toward Libby. "Come on, Lib. Do it."

Libby's heart raced as she tentatively punched in the number and waited. She held her breath and listened to one ring, then another. She'd almost given up when he finally answered.

"MacKenzie here." Cash's telephone voice had a deep, masculine note, precisely as she remembered it. The sting of his abandonment gripped her heart with fresh intensity, as though it had happened yesterday.

The assault on her confidence startled her and she nearly dropped the phone. Her mind suddenly went blank. She squeezed her eyes shut, reluctant to expose the deepest part of her to someone who hadn't cared back then and wouldn't now.

Holy Spirit, please, she prayed, *I need Your help! Give me the right words to say to him!*

Medley gave her a gentle nudge, pressuring her to speak.

She took a deep breath and opened her eyes. "Hello, Cash."

End of Excerpt

A note from Denise

Thank you so much for reading *Always is not Forever.* If you enjoyed this story, please take a moment to post a rating or short review at the retailer where you purchased it. Thank you! I appreciate it very much! Ratings and/or reviews help me to reach more people who love to read sweet romance. To be notified when a new book is available, be sure to follow me by signing up at:

https://www.deniseannettedevine.com/newsletter

More Books by Denise Devine

Christmas Stories
Merry Christmas, Darling

A Christmas to Remember

A Merry Little Christmas

A Very Merry Christmas - Hawaiian Holiday Series

~*~

Bride Books
The Encore Bride

Lisa – Beach Brides Series

Ava – Perfect Match Series

Della – *Coming Soon!*

~*~

Moonshine Madness Series - Historical Suspense/Romance
The Bootlegger's Wife – Book 1

Guarding the Bootlegger's Widow – Book 2

The Bootlegger's Legacy – Book 3

~*~

West Loon Bay Series – Small Town Romance
Small Town Girl – Book 1
Brown-Eyed Girl – Book 2
Country Girl – Book 3 - *Coming Soon!*

~*~

Christmas in West Loon Bay Series– Small Town Romance
Once Upon a Christmas – Book 1
Mistletoe and Wine – Book 2

~*~

Girl Friday Cozy Mystery Series
Shot in the Dark – Book 1
The Accidental Detective – *Coming Soon!*

Other Cozies
Unfinished Business
Dark Fortune

~*~

Forever Yours Series - Inspirational romance
Always is not Forever – Book 1
This Time Forever – Book 2

Want more? Read the first chapter of my novels or get my complete book list at:

https://deniseannette.blogspot.com

Passionate about sweet romance?

Want to be part of a fun group?

Visit us on Facebook at:

https://www.facebook.com/groups/denisedevinereadergroup

Audiobooks Galore!

Do you like audiobooks? Many in the list above are available in audio!
Check out Denise's website for links to each audiobook.

https://www.deniseannettedevine.com

Narrated by Lorana L. Hoopes

Monthly sales!

Made in United States
Orlando, FL
25 November 2024

54422805R00102